COMPLETE
BOOK OF ASPEN

DNA Sucks at Keeping Secrets

Danna Smith

PLUMBAGO PRESS | WOODBRIDGE CA

Plumbago Press
P.O. Box 101
Woodbridge, CA 95258
www.plumbagopress.com

Publisher's Note: This is a work of fiction. Names, characters, places, and incidents are a product of the author's imagination. Locales and public names are sometimes used for atmospheric purposes. Any resemblance to actual people, living or dead, or to businesses, companies, events, institutions, or locales is entirely coincidental.

Interior format by Danna Smith with Book Design Template
Book cover design by Book Cover Zone
The text of this book is set in Garamond

The Complete Book of Aspen/ Danna Smith. -- 1st ed.
ISBN 978-0-578-33248-2
ISBN 978-0-578-33249-9 e-book
Library of Congress Control Number: 2022900127

To my sister, Laurie, who walked with me
through the storm.

DNA neither cares nor knows. DNA just is.
And we dance to its music.
—Richard Dawkins

THE
COMPLETE
BOOK OF ASPEN

PLUMBAGO PRESS

Prologue

My best friend, Sophie
says DNA stands for
deoxyribonucleic acid.
The genetic code
that determines
the why,
the what,
and the who
of every living thing.

Cells.
Nucleotides.
Double Helix.

Whatever.

All I've learned
is DNA sucks
at keeping
secrets.

Hospitals

I hate them.
Especially the one
that held Dad hostage for weeks.

He insisted on the place.
It's not that he liked the beige walls
or the sickening aroma of antiseptic,
but he refused to die at home.

The sound of the monitor
broke through the silence,
ticking off each heartbeat.

beep
beep
beep

I rested my head
against the chair back
and closed my eyes
to happy memories.

The day we went berry picking
and came home way after dark
with empty buckets
and tummy aches.

And the time Dad taught
four-year-old me about spitballs.

When I sent one
s a i l i n g
across the table,
it hit Dad in the forehead.

We giggled
until I peed my pants.
Mom put *Dad* in time out.

beep
beep
beep

Dad liked to call me
his little Italian sparrow,
his *piccola passera Italiana,*
but I never imagined
he would fly away.

I leaned over to kiss
the paper-thin skin
on his cheek.

Aspen, is that you?

I took his hand in mine.
I'm here, Dad.

beep
beep
beep

That's when he told me.
Take care of Mom, he whispered.

That's when I promised.
I will! I cried.

beep
beep
beeeeeeeeeeeep

Fourteen

I was fourteen
when the monster
grabbed hold of Dad
with its sharp,

a   g   d
j   g   e

teeth.

Cancer dined
on his pancreas,
chewed him up
from the inside out.

I was fourteen
when death's shadow
loomed over our family,
pitching us into darkness.

I was fourteen
when I made a promise
I had no business making,
and no clue how to keep.

Sunday Mourning

I'd never been to a funeral
and it felt wrong to start with Dad's.
Isn't a girl supposed to lose
a hamster
or a goldfish
before she graduates to people?

I tried to wrap my head around it—
a world without Dad—
but I couldn't manage it.

Before he got sick
he was running marathons,
making pottery,
and telling stupid dad jokes.

My Dad's sister,
Auntie Allison, took my hand
and led me to our seats.

I sat in the middle.
My mom, my older brother, Cooper,
and Auntie Allison on one side,

my best friend, Sophie,
and her parents on the other.

A sandwich of support.

The Funeral

Technically, it wasn't a funeral.
There was no casket.
No hearse.
No burial.
Dad wanted his ashes
at home, with us.

Mom called it
a Celebration of Life.

While Auntie Allison
shared memories of Dad,
I looked around the church.

Black clothes.
Gold crosses.
White wreaths.
Red-rimmed eyes.

Color me a skeptic,
but it looked
like a funeral to me.

Angel Wings

Some people say
a song,
a hymn,
a hum,
is important
at a funeral
to send
a loved one
to heaven
on angel wings.
My brother
started the song
with a shaky voice.
He sang low
about sweet chariots.
The rest of us
joined in
on the second chorus.
Looking back,
I wonder why
we did that.
Why did we
sing a song
that took Dad away
when we wanted him,
needed him,
right here on Earth?

Goodbye Kiss

After the song,
we mingled with mourners,
appetizers in one hand,
soggy tissues in the other.

Cooper tried to be strong,
saving his tears for later
when he was alone.

We plastered
fake smiles on our faces
while people hugged us
and said stuff like,
Peter Deluca was loved.
He was a good man.
I'm sorry for your loss.

I hated how everyone
talked about Dad
like he wasn't there.

I looked at his picture
between two crystal vases
filled with white lilies.
A breeze blew
through the window
and kissed my cheek.

He was there.
I could feel it.

Breakdown

Mom was losing it.
She refused to leave the house.

She tried to hide it,
but her puffy eyes
and weight loss
were a dead giveaway.

Cooper and I protected her.
We made excuses for her.
We kept quiet.

Friends assumed she was busy
taking a crash course
on single parenthood.

She slept a lot.
Mom looked so lost
lying in that big bed,
Dad's side empty,
like he just got up
to go for a run.

She lived in his t-shirts,
refusing to let me wash them.
His familiar scent was her only lifeline.

The Smell of Sadness

Every morning
before I left for school,
I made Mom's breakfast.

She picked at her eggs
but I knew she'd dump them
the minute I left the house.

Our roles had officially reversed.

She reeked of sadness
or maybe it was the vodka.

Mom used to have a drink
or two
with dinner,
or at a party,
but after Dad died,
cocktail time was all the time.

Checked Out

Before long,
Mom lost her job at the CPA office.
She quit the garden club.
She quit her friends.
She quit eating and showering most days,
hell, she even quit Cooper and me.

It didn't happen overnight,
but by the time Dad's ashes
were delivered to our fireplace mantle,

Mom had completely checked out.

Sunshine

When I was
a little girl, my mom used
to sing that old song to me,"You
are my sunshine." She'd sing and
I'd hum along.But really, my mom is
my sunshine when skies are gray. An
ever-warm, ever-bright,ever-present light
in my life. She's brilliant, consistent, and
strong. Whenever my world went dark,
I could look for Mom, shining bright,
guiding me through the storm. Maybe
that's why it was so hard for me
to watch the light inside her
slowly fade out.

Hard Pass

My phone chimed with texts from friends.

Aspen, are you okay?
Want to grab a pizza?
My treat!

A flutter of excitement
grew in my belly
at the thought of joining them,
but it was always a hard pass.

I worried about leaving Mom
home alone for long.

I went to school
and for quick jogs
but I needed to stay close.

My life had to take a number.
Mom came first.

I had promised Dad.

After a while,
my friends stopped texting.
Except for Sophie, of course.

Bookends

Sophie and I
have been best friends
since before we could read.

We met at the library
during storytime.
Now, we're always together,
like bookends.

Every Saturday,
Sophie's Dad makes
homemade tamales.

Every Saturday,
after Mom's breakdown,
Sophie was at our door with dinner.

A whiff of toasted cumin
drew us into the kitchen.

That's my Sophie.
Her family is from Mexico,
but she jokes she's part Italian
like my dad and me.

I guess that makes us
something like sisters.

Unbreakable Bond

One night when we were ten,
Sophie and I watched a movie.
Two boys pricked their fingertips
with a pocketknife.

When they pressed
their bleeding fingers together,
they became brothers.

Blood brothers.

We were determined
to become blood sisters—
minus the pain.

We dipped our fingers
in ketchup,
performed the ritual,
drip
drip
drip
fingertip to fingertip.

And just like that
we were blood sisters,
or as we later joked,
ketchup sisters.

Either way,
we continue to share
an unbreakable bond.

Dad Sad

There are all kinds of sad.
Bad Grade Sad.
Break Up Sad.
World Problem Sad.

And then there's Dad Sad—
that's the sad that holds on
the longest and hurts the deepest.

You can't hurry
a thing like grief,
it takes its own sweet time.

Sometimes late at night,
when I heard Mom crying,
I crawled into her bed
and wrapped my arms around her.

It'll be okay
It'll be okay.
I repeated.

I don't know
if my nighttime chants
were for my mom or me.

All the While

While   friends met for burgers,
a sink full of food-caked
dishes met me.
With Auntie Allison's
long-distance assistance
and Sophie's visits,
I learned simple recipes.
Good enough to get by.
Not that any of us
had much of an appetite.

While   friends rode their bicycles
to the store to buy
a new pair of jeans
or a swimsuit
for a beach party,
I was stuck
running the spin cycle.
The laundry doesn't wash itself.

While   friends snuck alcohol
from their parent's cabinets,
I was holding my mom's hair back
while she puked up gin. A tonic
she thought would make her happy
but it always got the last laugh.

Migration

With Dad's insurance payout
and Mom's passwords,
Cooper kept our bills paid.

He never complained
but I could see the strain
of our new normal
in the sagging of his shoulders.

As time went on,
he didn't spend much time at home.
He liked staying at his friend's house
where he soaked up normalcy
like sunshine.

He reminded me
of the monarch butterflies
that migrate to our town every fall.
They handle their difficult journey
by using the sun to stay on course.

Cooper is an artist like Dad.
Not a potter, but a painter,
oils mostly.

He was a senior
on track to earning
a full-ride scholarship
to Columbia —his dream college.

Just like the Monarch,
Cooper migrated to a safe place,
so, in the end,
he could reach his destination.

I didn't blame him.
Dreams came to our house to die.

Birthday with Side Effects

Paxil
Zoloft
Xanax
Mom's doctors
kept changing her meds,
trying to find the magic solution.
The remedy that would
bring her back to us.

My fifteenth birthday
marked the six-month
anniversary of Dad's death.

Mom had been gone
for almost as long.

Her latest medication
came with unwanted side effects—
dizziness,
irritability,
forgetting your daughter's birthday.

Bibliotherapy

Every night before bedtime,
Mom and I would
squeeze
into Dad's recliner
and I would read to her.

We started a long fantasy series
but Mom couldn't focus
or keep the characters straight.

Before I was a chapter in,
she'd be snoring
or drooling
or both.

I'd fill in the blanks the next day.

By the time
we cracked open the fifth book,
Mom's concentration was improving.
Sometimes she even read to me.

Things were starting to look up.

Fast Forward

Eight months ago, when Dad died,
it almost killed us all
but we survived.

When I hear Mom's soft steps
and the shower sputter to life,
I stir from my musings.

I pad barefoot to the sink
with my cold coffee
and smile at the bundle
of sweet peas on the windowsill.

I knew Mom had come back to us
the day I found her in the garden
up to her elbows in dirt, weeping.

Not for Dad this time
but for her neglected begonias.
Look at what I've done! She cried.

I kneeled beside her
and picked up the pruning shears.
It's okay, Mom, I said, *I'll help*.

She got her job back
and signed up for a yoga class.

She's still hurting.
We all are.
But we're healing.

Mom is going to lunch with a friend today,
Cooper is away at college,
and I plan to hang out with Sophie.

I'd say, life is good,
but I don't want to jinx it.

DNA Kits

Sophie is obsessed with science,
she gobbles it up
like dark chocolate.

This month in biology
she's studying genetics.

Two DNA kits spill
from her backpack.
She holds one out to me,
It will be fun, she says.
Do it for science.

Spitting into a tube
isn't my idea of fun.
*Police catch criminals
with tests like these*, I say.

Have you committed a crime, Aspen? She smiles.

No, I laugh, *but a girl should keep her options open.*

                              air
                    the
              into
Sophie tosses the kit

                        and I catch it.

Mad Scientist

The boxes
contain everything
needed to test our DNA.
They remind me of the chemistry kit
Sophie received for her ninth birthday.
I stayed overnight after her party
and watched her turn into
a mad scientist,
measuring
and mixing
until midnight.

Some things
never
change.

Spitless

In my room,
we slide the tubes
from their boxes.

I fill mine
halfway to the line
before I'm out of spit.

Sophie grins.
Should I call Charlie?
You've been drooling over him.

I wish, I say, *he's working tonight.*

I believe the saying,
opposites attract.

My new boyfriend and I
are completely different
but we totally work.

He's the senior to my sophomore.
The tall to my short.
The calm to my storm.

I lift the tube
and try again.
No.
More.
Spit.

Sophie starts talking
about cheesy pizza,
pasta with marinara,
and spicy meatballs.

before long,
my mouth is watering.

You're a genius! I laugh,
capping the tube.

And now I'm starving!

Drop Box

On the way
to Enzo's restaurant, we
d
r
o
p
our DNA samples
into the big, blue mailbox.
Its metal mouth
gaping
on rusted hinges,
grinning,
like it knows
what we're up to.

Close Call

When I get home,
my mom is watching a movie,
our puppy, Nova,
curled up on her lap.

She invites me to sit,
patting the cushion beside her.

That's when I see it.
My empty DNA test box.

Mom looks at me suspiciously,
I found this in the garbage.
Is it yours?

I can't admit it's mine.
I lied about my age to take it.

Mom hates liars.

Luckily, Sophie kept her box.
Sophie took the test, I say.
You know how obsessed she is with science.

Worry

If worrying were a sport,
my mom would be
Olympic qualified.

She warms up
by saying DNA tests
are big trouble
and moves toward a roster
of concerns in record time.

> Sophie's DNA could
> become public knowledge.

> It can be used against her,
> on the job
> and with the law.

> Her results could
> be sold to strangers.

I'm glad you didn't take a test, Mom says.

A knot forms in my stomach.
If she only knew.

Mixed Nuts

We watch the rest
of the movie together
sharing a blanket
and a bag of chocolate almonds.

I can't stop thinking
about my DNA test.

I ask Mom where she's from.
She says her family genes
are like a can of mixed nuts,
Irish,
French,
British,
German,
Swedish.

I guess that makes me
mixed nuts too.
But I'm also Italian, like my dad.

Confession

I check my email every day.
Twice a day.
Sometimes three times.

I have a secret
not even Sophie knows
because I'm afraid
to say the words out loud.

My family tree
isn't the only thing
that has me curious.
My spit will also be tested
for genetic mutations.

Did Dad have a gene
that gave him cancer?
Grandma Deluca died of cancer too.

Did I inherit that gene?

If I did
and if I know about it,
maybe I can prevent it.

Maybe cancer won't eat me up
like it did them.

Maybe.

A Girl's Gotta **Work**

I got a job at the library.
Every Friday after school
I shelve books,

putting them back in order where they belong.

When I step into the library,
I see friendly locals
and a few wandering souls
resting and reading in recliners
bathed in shafts of sunlight.

A mountain of books
heaped on a cart
waits for me.

I coax the wobbly cart
to the biography section
and spend the next four hours
among friends.

Aristotle to Zappa.

Book Love

Books have always held
a special magic
with the power to pull me in.

I flip through the pages,
scanning passages,
skimming paragraphs,
studying pictures.

If there were a book about me,
I wonder what the title would be.

Girl Running

Italian Sparrow

The Complete Book of Aspen

If I found my biography
right here,
right now,
I would flip to the end.
I would want to know
how my life played out.

Mrs. Dunn,
the librarian, clears her throat.
You're getting paid to shelve books, Aspen, not read them.

Busted.

I slide Einstein into his proper place.

I'm down to six books
when I get Charlie's text.
His shift at Java Junkie has ended.

Pick u up at 8.

Bonfire Victories

Football victories
and bonfires
go together like
chocolate,
marshmallows
and graham crackers.

On the nights
after a home game win,
students blow onto the beach
like a swift sea breeze.

We search the shore for kindling,
claim logs from truck beds,
and strike a match,
watching our worries
of teachers,
tests,
and tomorrows

                          flames.
                  in
      up
go

At least for a little while.

Hot Date

Salty sea breezes
and floating embers
mingle in the night sky.

Halsey is singing
about putting on a show
through a speaker
somewhere in the dark.

Charlie smiles
and takes my hand
as we weave our way
through a sea of party goers.

Charlie has an amazing smile,
I told him so one day.

That's not the only amazing thing, he winked,
and then he kissed me
right there
in our own little corner
of the school cafeteria.

If anyone ever tells you
that you can't fall in love
with a guy
you have only known
for three months,
they don't know Charlie.

Jaxon

We find Sophie
sitting on a blanket
with other brainiacs
from the science club.

Jaxon Lee and a group of jocks
sit on a blanket nearby.

I don't know much about Jaxon
except that he's a track star
at the private school, Cliff Academy.

He introduces himself,
says he's seen me hitting the trails
after school and on weekends.

I've seen him running too.

While I talk to Jaxon,
Charlie inches closer
and puts his arm around me.
I lean into his warmth.

If I didn't know better,
I'd think he was jealous.

Jaxon asks me
if I run track at my school.
I shake my head.

The truth is,
I started running alone
after Dad died.

The last time I checked,
grieving was not a team sport.

Kisses

We leave the crowd behind
for a walk on the beach.

Charlie reaches
into his jacket pocket.
Close your eyes.

He places something
in the palm of my hand.
I try to guess what it is.

It's small and smooth.
Not a seashell
or a pebble.

I peek.
Chocolate? I smile.

I have a sweet tooth, Charlie laughs,
revealing a handful
of silver-wrapped treats.

He sits down in the sand,
pulls me onto his lap,
and shares his kisses.

The chocolate kind
and the boyfriend kind.

The Best Kind of Math

The next day we're eating pizza
and as I watch Charlie
inhale his third piece,
I'm reminded of the day we met.

When my new math tutor
knocked on my door,
all green eyes,
blond curls,
and killer biceps,
I thought I was in heaven.

Then one day,
he shared his pizza with me
and I knew I was in heaven.

He asked me out a week later.
We've been together ever since.

Charlie + Pizza = Love

One Hundred Percent

When we've eaten all the pizza,
we start on the bonus cheesy bits
stuck to the cardboard box.

Nova stands watch,
licking her lips
hoping a crumb will tumble.

Charlie "accidentally"
drops a crisp pepperoni.

Damn it, he grins.

Charlie has an early shift
so I walk him out to his car.

You're the cutest barista ever! I say.
That's why they pay me the big bucks, he jokes.

Charlie pours every dollar
he makes at the coffee house
into his Mustang.
He rebuilt the engine,
but it's still a rust bucket.
He's saving to have it repainted.

Before we say goodbye,
I remember to tell him
that I took a DNA test.

He says if he took a DNA test
he'd be 50% coffee
and 50% Pennzoil.

He always knows
how to make me laugh.

Charlie is 100% amazing.

Mom and Me

I try to meet up with Sophie
but she's away, busy being brilliant
at a science club competition.

So, when Mom asks me
if I want to grab some lunch,
I'm already out the door.

By the time we choose a seat
outside at Luna's,
I'm ready to dive
into a bowl
filled deep
as
the
ocean
with creamy clam chowder.

Mom hands the wine list
back to the server.
I'll have iced tea.

While we wait for our soup,
we laugh at the names
of sailboats anchored in the water.

Pier Pressure
Piece of Ship
Buoyance'

I'm tapping my spoon
to the
beat
beat
beat
of a Beach Boy's song
when Mom sees the flower
inked in shades of pink
on my wrist.

Nice tattoo, she says.

Sophie drew it with a gel pen, I say.

Mom smiles. *Sophie's a good artist.*

I look at my mom, smiling,
in the warm September sunshine
and I thank God she came back to us.

I missed her.

She's a good mom,
funny,
smart,
not always on my butt
about everything.

If I were in trouble
she would be there for me
in a heartbeat.

I look at my wrist and decide
when I turn eighteen,
I'm getting a real tattoo.

Of a heart.

And I'll convince Mom
to get one to match.

Freaky

I'm painting my toenails
when Sophie calls, shouting
Turn on the TV!

A news story
about DNA disasters.

We watch the show together,
separately,
amazed at the test discoveries.

Two childhood friends
who were neighbors,
turned out to be brothers.

One woman learned
her parent's fertility doctor
was her father.
She has eighteen siblings!

Another woman found
her older sister was really
her mother.

That's freaky! I say.
But those are rare cases.

I think again of the possibility
of inheriting cancer
through my genes.

I hope we get our results soon, I say.

Me too, Sophie laughs.
Maybe I'll find out I'm a twin separated at birth!

Digging

I'm in Dad's studio
above the garage
doing geology homework
and digging up good memories.

When I was little,
I liked *Beauty and the Beast*.
I used to wear my Princess Belle dress
and dance around Dad while he worked.
Together, we'd sing, *Be Our Guest*.

I loved watching him
throw a bowl or vase.
He made it look so easy.

He'd smack the clay down
and set the wheel
spin
spin
spinning.

His hands were magic,
squeezing,
pulling,
pressing.

Dad had a knack for turning
a beastly lump of clay
into a beauty.

Forget Me Not

Dad now rests
on our fireplace mantel
in a golden glazed urn,
etched with Forget-me-Nots.

One day, Cooper and I found Dad
crouched over his wheel,
dark circles
under sunken eyes.

My home, he said.
When the monster takes its

last bite.

My Studio Now

Mom kept Dad's studio
just the way he left it
so I could be a potter, too.

I was learning to throw,
taking lessons from Dad
on weekends until he got sick.
We were going to work together.

Artistic talent
runs in my family.
Sculpting.
Photography.
Painting.

I try,
but I'm pretty sure
the artsy gene skipped me.

Mom says I just need
more practice.

I want to make Dad proud,
so I pull out some clay,
push in my earbuds,
and set the wheel spinning
like a carousel,
hoping my talent
jumps on for a ride.

Results for Breakfast

A big breakfast
is a Saturday morning ritual
at Sophie's house.

Sophie's mom
hands us each a basket
and shoos us out the door.
I stand on tiptoes,
Sophie crouches
beneath branches
as we twist
and
pull
sweet oranges
ripe for juicing.

We're working on
a serious stack of pancakes
when Sophie's phone dings.

Her test results are in!

I peek over her shoulder.
Pie charts
and country maps
paint the screen
a rainbow of colors,
purple,
red,
blue,
outlining her ethnic background,

Spanish,
British,
Irish,
Native American,
African.

What, no Italian? I tease.

Check yours! Sophie laughs.

My battery is dead, I frown.
I forgot to charge it last night.

Sophie slides
her charger across the table,
then steals the last of the pancakes.

Take your time! She smiles.

Dead Phone

Plug in
Power up
Log on
Sign in
Scroll

d
o
w
n

No DNA results.

Pop Quiz

On Friday morning
I have a pop quiz in history class.

I warn Sophie at our locker.
She has history fourth period—
her least favorite subject.

Mr. Chu is out to get us, she says.
I'm going to fail, big time!

We swap the books in our backpacks
for books in our locker,
rotating them
like tires in a pit stop.

I look at the time on my phone.
I can't be late again.

How'd you do on the quiz? Sophie asks.

Aced it! I say.

How about the other test? She asks.

I shrug. *No news yet.*

I make it to class on time
then take a quick look
back at Sophie.

She's standing in Mr. Chu's doorway
stabbing at her heart
with an invisible sword.

Death by history quiz.

Big News

While I'm shelving books,
Mother Nature is working too,
her fingers spreading fog
like polish on Mom's old silver tray.

When my shift is over,
Sophie walks in.
I have big news, she whispers.
I'll tell you on the ride home.

Sophie's pale blue VW Beetle
is a bright patch of summer sky
beneath the yellow glow
of the streetlamp.

When she turns the key in the ignition
Taylor Swift is singing
about being fifteen.

I turn up the volume
and we sing along,
except we change the lyrics
to *sixteen.*

Sophie already had a birthday
and mine is in November.

If I don't hear her news soon,
I'm afraid Sophie might explode.
I turn in my seat to face her,
Spill it!

Connections

Sophie's face glows with excitement,
Do you know Jasmine Garcia?

I can count the things I know
about Jasmine on one hand.

She's a junior at our school.
She has long pink hair.
A turquoise nose stud.
Her nickname is Jaz.
She plays the guitar.

Sophie found Jaz's name
on the DNA website
under her *family connections.*
It turns out they share
a great,
great,
grandmother.

I can't believe Jaz is your cousin! I say.

We're meeting up tomorrow, Sophie says.
Come with me?

She's stoked but nervous.
She didn't think she had family
in the states.

Grandma Deluca used to say
Good friends are harder to catch
than a shooting star.

Sophie was my strength
through my dad's death
and my mom's depression.
She fed me,
comforted me,
and made me laugh when happiness
felt as distant as the Milky Way.

Of course, I say.

She pulls in front of my house,
our deep blue door
barely visible
through the heavy mist.

See you tomorrow, I smile,
punching the lock on her door
and slamming it shut.

As I make my way
toward the beacon
of our porch light,
I wonder if *my* results

are lost at sea.

Nicknames

Jasmine has the best nickname
for a musician.

I get most nicknames,
Jaz for Jasmine
Soph for Sophie,
and Jax for Jaxon,
but Charlie's family calls him Chuck.

How do you get Chuck from Charlie?

My dad didn't like my name at first
because there isn't a nickname
for Aspen,
except for Ass
and what kind of nickname is that?

Still, my mom insisted
on naming me Aspen
and nobody calls me Ass.

At least not to my face.

Meeting Up

Sometimes families grow
in different directions
like the roots of a tree
but they are always connected.

When Sophie and I
step into Java Junkie,
the bell above the door tells on us.
Jaz looks up and waves.

Charlie's behind the counter
sipping on free coffee,
looking as hot as ever.

When he hands us our drinks,
he winks at me.
See you tonight!

I look at that beautiful guy
and wonder how I got so lucky.

We sit at a table
overlooking Main Street,
fall leaves littering the busy sidewalk.

Sophie and Jaz
never spoke at school,
but they hit it off immediately.

They talk about
the adventures of a relative
who's into extreme mountain biking.

I half-listen,
sipping my caramel macchiato,
feeling like a third wheel.

Running Partner

I wake up early
to Nova nudging my hand.

I know what I'll find
before I open my eyes,
a wagging whiptail,
and a leash clenched
between sharp teeth.

I clip the leash to her collar
and pull on yesterday's sweats.

I have a horrible habit
of letting the screen door bang shut.

Don't slam the door! Mom shouts
from the bench in the garden.

Too late.

Palm trees line the street
waving to us as we pass
on our way to the dog park.

Nova's buddy Diesel,
a pit bull with a perpetual smile,
is there to greet her.

I'm reaching into my backpack
for doggy treats when I see Jaxon.

Which dog is yours? I ask.

He points to a German shepherd
with a coat the color of honey.
That's Hunter, he says.

We sit side by side,
watching the dogs play.

We should run together sometime, Jaxon says.

I hesitate,
wondering if Charlie will mind.
But no, it's not a date.
It's just running.

Cyclone

Sophie, Jaz, and I are outside
exchanging school gossip
when the wind picks up.

Crisp leaves leap
from the ground,
swirling
into a colorful cyclone.

A dizzy of yellow.
A busy of red.

We laugh,
running for cover.
The screen door slams behind us,
trapping the storm outside.

We're retreating to my bedroom
with mugs of hot chocolate
when my phone chimes.

I've Got Mail

To: runninggirl@email.com
From: donotreply@my-dna.org
Subject: DNA results

Your DNA results are in.
View your reports now.

My breath catches,
my heart races,
my finger hovers over the link.

C l i c k !

First Things First

I go straight
to the wellness section
and click on *carrier status*.

The reports show
variants were detected
for a few minor health conditions.

If variants are found
there is an increased chance
of getting the condition.

I scroll down
and find a cancer
predisposition link.

Before I can read the report,
I'm required to acknowledge
that I understand...

> I understand the test doesn't look
> for all types of cancer.
> *Click.*

> I understand if variants are detected,
> it doesn't mean I'll get cancer.
> *Click.*

> I understand I can still get cancer
> even if no variants are found.
> *Click.*

The blue circle icon
on my phone spins
around
and around
loading my data
like it's holding its breath.

A new window
pops up on my screen.

[No Known Variant.]

I sag with relief.

I'm not playing a game
and this test result
isn't a get-out-of-jail-free card.
But I feel better knowing
I don't carry the hideous monster gene
that gobbled up Dad and Grandma.

So, Sophie says. *What does it say?*
Are we sisters?

I click on my ancestry report.

Let's find out, I laugh.

Genetic Breakdown

I make my way down
the list.
British
Irish
Greek
Swedish
French
German

I reread the list.

I'm mixed nuts for sure.
But Italian?

Not.
One.
Drop.

That last thought
plays in my mind,
again
and again,
like the needle
stuck in a groove
on one of Mom's old records.

No Italian.
No Italian.
No Italian
No Italian?

Sophie notices my trembling hands
and rushes to my side.
What's wrong? she asks as I sit down.

When I share my results, she gasps.

Aspen! Were you adopted?

DNA (Do Not Assume)

The thing is,
I know my dad was Italian.

The Deluca lineage
has been traced
and documented.

Our family tree
is hanging on our wall.
Not to mention
Dad's major accent
and the shoebox
spilling over
with records
of his Italian ancestors.

Jaz looks over my shoulder,
34.2% Greek?
Where did that come from?

I stare at the results.

It must be a mistake.

Mistakes Happen

Maybe   the lab tech
                     sneezed in my sample,
                     messing up my results.

I'm   pretty sure my spit
                     is defective.

The   charts are complicated,
                     easy to misinterpret.

Mistake   or no mistake,
                     that is the question.
                     Do I want to know the
                     answer?

Revelation

I think about my brother.
Cooper is the spitting image of Dad
right down to the square jaw
and the goofy walk.

Me, not so much.

Come to think of it,
I'm the only one
in my family with dimples.

I know I wasn't adopted.
I've seen pictures
of Mom pregnant with me,
a young Cooper in her arms.

My sonogram
stamped "Baby Girl Deluca"
is glued in my scrapbook.

I look at Sophie and Jaz.

Nobody wants to say it.
But we're all thinking
the same thing.

My dad was not my father.

Storm

A storm is brewing,
batten down the ship's hatches,
here come all the waves.

Fun

If fun means
your whole world
turns upside down
like you're riding a

RoLLeRcOaSTeR

that you weren't tall enough
to ride in the first place.
And now you're sick
and scared
and regret
walking through
the entrance gate
on
tip
toes
then Sophie was right,
taking a DNA test was a blast!

Stupid Test

Sophie feels rotten.
Stupid test!
Stupid me for buying it.
It was all my idea!
Will you ever forgive me?

I hug her.
I don't blame you, Soph.

I'm pissed.
There's only one person to blame.

Mom

The sky is glazed
a deep shade of amber
as I wait for my mom in the garden.

Emotions are prickling
inside me like angry thorns.

She drives up
with a trunk full of groceries.
Give me a hand, will you?

I don't move from the bench.
We need to talk, I say.

Mom frowns. *Is everything okay?*

I look at her
and tears flood my eyes.

Aspen, you're scaring me!

I bite my lip.
Shake my head.

Everything is definitely not okay.

Overboard

When I tell Mom
I took a DNA test, she gasps
like a woman drowning.

She panics,
looking around for a float
or a rope
to save her.

I almost feel sorry for her
but I can tell by the look
on her face,

it's true.

My dad was *not* my father.

Duel

Me: *I'm not Italian.*
Her: *Of course, you are!*
Me: *My DNA says I'm Greek.*
Her: *Those tests are always wrong.*
Me: *Said no one ever!*
Her: *Drop it, Aspen.*
Me: *Who is my father?*
Her: *Peter Deluca was your father!*
Me: *My other father, Mom!*
Her: *Don't be ridiculous.*

Mom folds her arms across her chest,
My personal life is none of your business.

She turns and walks away.

Seriously?

I don't know
what I expected Mom to say
but it wasn't, "None of your business."

How could you do this to me? I cry.

She lifts a grocery bag,
and then another,
threading her arm
through the handles.

I told you to drop it, Aspen.

I follow her
up the porch steps,
angry words erupting
from my mouth
like lava
from a volcano.

What is wrong with you? I shout.
My entire life has been a lie!

Mom looks around,
lowers her voice,
*I will not have you
poking around in my past.*

I take a step closer,
raise my voice,

It's not about your past, Mom,
it's about my future.
I have a right to know who I am!

This time,
it's Mom who slams the door.

Painful

Since I was a little girl,
I've built my life
around what my
mom told me.
My identity,
security,
and self-worth,
depended
on that information.
There is nothing
more painful,
nothing,
than learning
the person you love
and trust most
in the world
has betrayed you.

Night Run

I burst
out of the house
like it's on fire.

I can't take one more
suffocating breath
inside those walls
with my mom.

Today I lost my dad
for a second time.

I just want the truth
but the truth is,
Mom isn't talking.

The moon
guides me to the beach
in streams of soft light.

I usually run
to find happiness
but it laps ahead of me tonight.

An old piece of driftwood
invites me to sit.

I wipe a mixture
of tears and snot
on the sleeve of my hoody
and listen to the restless ocean whisper,

    If your dad isn't your real dad,
            does that mean you aren't his real daughter?

Calling all Friends

Charlie sleeps with his phone
under his pillow.

His mom has been known
to sneak into his room
at night
and collect it
like a lost tooth
without leaving him a dime.

So when he doesn't answer,
I'm not worried.

I call Sophie next.
When she doesn't pick up,
I text her.

I talked to Mom.

She replies,
@at movie with Jaz
leaving now

I text back
telling her to stay
that I'm okay for tonight.

I can't tell Cooper
or Auntie Allison,
it would break their hearts.

I stare at my phone,
and sigh.

There is no one else to call.

Layers of Paint

Back home,
I'm not ready to go inside.

                              studio
                         the
                    to
               steps
          the
     climb
I

When I open
the arched door,
the sweet smell
of nostalgia greets me.

The loft is stuffed
to the rafters
with bristly brushes,
pints of old glaze,
and unfinished pottery—
frozen in time.

A box of clay sits on a shelf.

Is that what I am?
A lump of clay
for my mom to mold
into anything she sees fit.

A person can't just decide
that a mug is a bowl,
a plate is a vase,
or a girl is a Deluca.

It is what it is.
No amount of pretending
will change the facts.

Years ago,
Mom made a choice
to paint over reality.

Her deception is opaque
but the truth has been there
all along
beneath layers
and layers
of pretty paint.

I know the real reason
my mom isn't talking.

When the truth gets out,
everyone is going to see
her true colors.

Italian My Ass

I slip inside the house
through the kitchen slider,
quiet as a secret.

The lights are out.
Nova's claws ticking
on the tile, the only sound.

Heading to the sink
for a drink of water,
I pass our family tree.

I yank it off the wall
and hurl it into the trash can.

The glass s h a t t e r s.

Sinking to the floor,
I pull Nova onto my lap.
Her soft, white fur
soaks up my tears.

One day I came home from a run
with a wet puppy tucked
inside my jacket.

I found her shivering
on the beach,
sand clinging like hope
to the hungry little dog.

I named her Nova
after my favorite superhero.
I rescued her.
She rescued me.

Later we found out
she's an Italian greyhound
boxer mix.

And then it hits me,
right there on the kitchen floor.

My dog is more Italian than I am!

Now I'm laughing
and crying
at the same time.

Just Kidding

Steam wraps its arms
around me in a warm hug
and I try to relax.

I stare into Dad's shaving mirror
still suction-cupped
to the shower wall.
A stranger looks back.
She's a fool!

All her life, she believed
what her mother told her
only to now hear, *just kidding.*

> *You have his eyes,*
> *just kidding.*

> *You're Italian,*
> *just kidding.*

> *He's your father,*
> *just kidding.*

I step out of the shower
sagging from heat
and heartbreak.

It'll be okay, Mom, I whisper,
I can forgive you.

> *Just kidding.*

Dreaming?

With my dark hair still damp
and tangled in knots,
I fall into bed, exhausted.

I've grown a lot
since Dad called me
his little sparrow.
Still, this burden is too heavy
for my fragile wings.

This is the kind of thing
that happens to other people.

I pull my quilt up to my chin
and close my eyes,
but sleep doesn't come.

Maybe I'm already asleep
and any minute now,
I'm going to jolt awake
to find the sandman
has punked me.

Under the covers,
I pinch myself
to see if I'm dreaming.

Damn it, that hurt.

Selfie

I look at the picture beside my bed.
It makes me smile—
even on the worst days.

A selfie of Cooper and me
at the airport,
before he left for college.

I told him to smile
on the count of three,
but he stuck out his tongue instead.

When he isn't annoying me
he's a cool big brother.

Which reminds me,
I should tell Cooper about the test.

Calling Cooper

It's 11:04 p.m. in California,
2:04 a.m. in New York
at Cooper's art school.
He might still be awake
studying,
or painting,
or partying.

I dial his number.
My call goes to voice mail.

Yo, Coop here, leave a message.

It's good to hear his voice
but I don't leave a message.

How do you tell a person
you're a counterfeit sister
in thirty seconds after a beep?

I shoot him a quick text
saying I butt-dialed him
so he doesn't call me back.

I'll share the news
when he comes home for the holidays.

Merry Christmas, we've been duped!

How's that for a Hallmark greeting?

The Next Morning

Just as I thought,
Tooth Fairy Mom
was at it again.

Charlie found his phone
on the kitchen table,
the mailbox full
of frantic messages
from yours truly.

He calls me
on the last charge of his battery,
Aspen, what's wrong?

Everything! I say.
Can you come over?

I'm halfway there.

Keepsakes

I keep memories of Dad
in a cookie tin under my bed.

While I wait for Charlie,
I dump the contents out
on my quilt.

> A shark's tooth we found
> on the beach after a storm.

> An origami crane
> Dad taught me how to fold.

> His high school class ring,
> still too big for my finger.

> A spare key to the art studio.

> A magic quarter.

> Birthday cards.

> Pictures.

Fossils of a father.

Charlie to the Rescue

When I hear a knock,
I open the door and

f
a
l
l

into Charlie's arms
like a rag doll.

Hey, he says, holding me close,
What happened?

Between sobs and hiccups,
I tell Charlie
e v e r y t h i n g.

He takes my hand
and leads me to the couch.
Shhhh, he whispers.

He gently raises my chin
until I'm looking
into his kind eyes.
Love makes a family, Aspen, not DNA.
Peter was your dad.

If anybody knows about families,
it's Charlie.

He was adopted
when he was three years old.

One time, I asked him
if he ever wanted
to see his real mom.

He said his adoptive mom
is his real mom,
and he sees her
every
single
day.

Differences

I understand
where Charlie is coming from
but our circumstances are different.

His biological parents were druggies
who'd rather chase a high
than a toddler.

Child Protective Services
rescued him from a life of neglect.

His new parents wanted him
with
all
their
hearts.

They *chose* him.

My mom's secrecy
stole my choice
like a sneaky thief.

I deserve the truth.
My Dad deserved the truth.
My biological father does too.

It might have been messy for Mom,
but the way I see it,
three truths are better than a lie.

There's This Guy

His name
is Rube Goldberg
and he's ruining my life.

When Sophie
doesn't return my call
about my talk with Mom,
I text her.

She replies
saying she's helping Jaz
with her Rube Goldberg project
for physics class.

Rube was an engineer,
cartoonist,
and inventor.

Jaz has to build
a complex machine
with pulleys
and levers
using rulers,
toilet paper rolls,
springs,
and other things
like in Rube's cartoons.

The project reminds me
of a board game
we used to play.

A ball rolled down a chute,
      passed through a sequence
         of chain reactions,
            causing a trap to fall,
                on a mouse.

Sophie promises
we'll talk later
but I'm not holding my breath.

She may be a genius at inventions
but she hasn't mastered
the telephone yet.

Curiosity

There is a large
freckle on the bottom of my
foot like a period at the end of a
sentence. Does my biological father
have   freckles too?
                                  Does his hair
                                  frizz on rainy
                                  days? Are his
                                  second toes
                                  longer than
                                  the others?
                                  Do we have
                                  the same
                                  blood type?
                                  Is he left-
                                  handed?
                                  I have a
                                  million
                                  questions!
                                  If curiosity
                                  killed the
                                  cat, it is

                                  definitely
                                  my fault.

Rainy Days and Mondays

Sleep.
Toss
Turn
Wake up
Repeat

When my alarm rings at 6 a.m.
the rain is tapping out
a somber song on my window.

I lie in bed
willing myself to get up
and get dressed for school.

I'm tired.

Tired of being sad,
tired of being angry,
so damn tired of it all.

Mom's already at work.
Nobody will know
if I stay in bed.

I look at Nova —she's tired too.

I pull the covers
over our heads
and for the first time in my life,

I skip school.

Sophie the Spy

It's afternoon,
and I'm having a pity party in my room
(I brought the nachos).

Sophie is blowing up my phone
wondering why I wasn't
at school today.

She's been so busy
with her new cousin,
I'm surprised she noticed.

When I don't answer
she drives to my house.
She lets herself in
and finds me in bed
with my curtains closed.

You okay? she asks,
turning on the lamp.

I'm wearing my panda pajamas,
my hair poking out
in all directions.

I don't know who I am! I sigh.
How can I be okay?

Yes, you do! Sophie says,
crawling into bed beside me.

She says everything
I let into my life
makes me who I am.

The books I read,
the music I listen to,
the people I admire.

I get it, I say.
I'm more than the sum of my parts.
But if that's true, Sophie, why do I feel so incomplete?

Sophie sighs.
Then there's only one thing to do.
You have to find your biological father.

I think about that.
Does finding my biological father
mean losing my mom?
Would I be betraying the dad who raised me?
Would it destroy my biological father's life?
Would it alienate me from my brother,
Auntie Alison, and the rest of the Delucas'?

Sophie wipes my tears away
with her thumbs,
Follow your heart.

Lost and Found

Sophie tugs me from my bed,
throws a rumpled t-shirt at me,
and tells me to get dressed.

She says she's taking me
to find my smile.

Apparently,
it's hiding in a bucket
of double chocolate fudge
at The Creamery.

I love that girl.

Ice Cream

Scoops of happiness
rolled up like somersaults on
crunchy quilted cones.

Just Another Day in Paradise

A sliver of morning sunlight
squeezes through
my bedroom curtains.

I open my eyes
to a nagging feeling
that something is wrong.

Then I remember
the tabloid talk show
my life has become.

I grab my laptop
and crawl back into bed
to check the DNA site for updates.

My family tree winks to life.
The branches have been
filled in automatically
based on the DNA
of family members.

I've added members too,
but without information
from both of my parents
my tree is lopsided.

Distant paternal cousins
have listed a long string
surnames on their profiles—

Hill
Strong
Papadakis
Burns
Spanos
Alanis
Davis

All dead ends.

I slam my laptop shut,
roll out of bed,
and shuffle down the hall
looking for Charlie's good friend,

coffee.

Early Birds

Mom's in the kitchen
slamming pots and pans
like it's a cool thing to do.

I pour myself a cup of coffee
and sit at the table
by the window.

I'm wearing the nightgown Mom hates.
It's "too sexy and inappropriate
for a girl my age."

Outside in the courtyard
early birds hop through hedges
looking for early worms.

Mom joins me at the table,
her coffee steaming
in a yellow happy face mug.

A happy face?
Talk about inappropriate.

She looks at me
and starts dropping excuses
like trees
                    drop

        autumn

                    leaves.

Excuses

I was lonely, she said,
vulnerable,
afraid of not being loved.

I told you only the good things
about your dad,
but he was distant,
always in his studio.

I felt like his art meant more to him
than I did.

I met a charming man,
a gentleman,
irresistible,
addictive,

married.

Spinning

My mind spins
with a million questions.

>How could Mom cheat on Dad?
>Where is "Prince Charming" now?
>Does he know I exist?
>Did Dad know I wasn't his?
>Wasn't I worth the truth?

But I ask only one question.
Just one.
The others can wait.

Who is my father?

The Keeper of Secrets

Mom is looking at me
like *I* did something wrong.

She says I need to stop prying
into her business.

> I say it became my business
> the minute I was conceived.

She says nobody else knows,
and she's not talking.

> I say my biological father
> and I have a right to know.

She says there are repercussions
to revealing secrets.

> I say there are repercussions
> to keeping secrets.

She says people will get hurt
if the truth comes out

> I say people are already hurting!

I might have a
living,
breathing,
father out there
somewhere.

I beg Mom,
Shine some light on this for me!

She says, *darkness suits me.*

Note to Self

You
can't
expect
a
person
to
shine
a
light
on
the
truth
when
they
are
benefiting
from
you
being
in
the
dark.

Akin

Last night,
Mom sent me to my room
like I'm a five-year-old.
She said I needed
to think about
what I had done,
digging up buried secrets,
bringing shame
and embarrassment
to the family.
If hatred isn't what I'm feeling
toward my mother right now,
it's a close relative.

Good Girl Gone Bad

What happens
when a good girl goes bad?

I'm asking for a friend.

Does her heart
curl up on the edges,
turn brown and whither?

Does her soul
grow rotten like fruit
left too long in the bowl?

This girl,
she was trusting,
a loving daughter.

Betrayal has filled her
with unfamiliar emotions.
Despair.
Anger.
Resentment.

She wonders,
do these feelings
make her a terrible person?

Or could it be that
the good girl hasn't gone bad?
Maybe she's just human.

Grim Thought

I'm lying in bed
wrapped in a quilt like a mummy
when a terrible thought hits me.

I find my mom on her yoga mat
in the lavender garden
and beg her for an answer.

Is this dad dead too?

Mom pauses mid-pose.
He's alive and well.

It Could be a Lie

When someone lies
everything
else
they
say,
everything,
becomes
questionable.
Everything
changes
when someone lies.

The Search Begins

Mom won't tell me anything
so it's up to me to find
my biological father.

I've never gambled in my life,
yet here I am willing to risk
everything
on the slim chance
that my biological father
will want anything to do with me.

I call Sophie, and an hour later
she's at my door with tacos
and an order of cheesy tots.

She hugs me,
says she can't stay long.

Any news about Bio-dad?

I laugh. *Bio-dad?*

What else are you going to call him, sperm donor?

No news yet, I say.
But I bet we can find some clues.

Mom collects things
from important events in her life.

Concert T-shirts.
Newspaper articles.
Pressed flowers.

Knowing her,
she's kept a keepsake
of her infidelity too.

Clean Socks Dirty Secrets

We check Mom's closet,
under the bed,
the hamper.

We open dresser drawers.
Scarves.
Nightgowns.
Underwear.

Nothing.

When Sophie peels back
a rose-scented drawer liner,
she yells out like it's game night
at summer camp.

Bingo!

Under the liner,
lies an envelope,
inside the envelope,

a picture.

Clue #1

The picture is old school.
The kind you shake
and an image magically appears.

Mom leans against Dad's red Jeep,
her blonde hair stuffed
beneath a beanie.

She's hugging a man
who's smiling
like he just won the lottery.

A note is scribbled
on the white strip
beneath the picture—

I love you, babe, Luke
February 2nd

I use my cell phone
to snap a picture
of the picture
then slide it back into the drawer.

Snooping didn't give me answers,
it only raised more questions.

Like who is Luke?
And how can I find him?

Photobomb

I've heard the saying,
a picture is worth
a thousand words.
If that's true,
a picture of my married mom
with her arms around a man
who is not my dad,
is a whole damn book!

R.I.P

I
never
thought
I'd
say
this,
but
I'M GLAD MY DAD IS ALREADY DEAD
because
if
he
knew
what
Mom
did
to
us
it
would
kill
him.

Time to Run

Hoping a long run
with tunes
pumping
in my ears
will make my problems

disappear,

I head toward the beach
passing kids with kites,
wind-kissed cheeks
raised toward the sky.

When I look past the pier,
I'm surprised to see Jaxon
running up ahead.

I pick up my pace,
z i p p i n g
past him with a head start,
Race you to the lighthouse!

I hear him close behind, laughing.
Then we're running side by side,
our feet pounding the sand
seriously in sync.

Cliffhanger

The land stops
so we do too.

We look down
from the edge of the cliff
at the crashing waves.

Seagulls struggle to fly
in the gusty wind.

Chugging from our water bottles,
we rest on the crumbling steps
of the ancient lighthouse.

Jaxon tells me he's been butting heads
with his dad lately.
His mom says they're too much alike.
I ask him about his mom,
he says they're tight.

I tell him my mom used to be chill.
He asks if Mom and I
are butting heads.

I nod.
Something like that.

Flesh and Blood

With the sun
setting its sights
on bedtime
and wildflowers
preparing to close
for the night,
we say goodbye.

It's been cool
getting to know Jaxon.

He's easy to talk with.
He's cute too.
Chiseled.
Lean.
Like a Renaissance sculpture.
Only he's flesh and blood
and wearing running shorts.

Replaced

I hear the music
long before I jog
around the corner.

Jaz stands in the garden
at Hype Café
strumming on her guitar.

Sophie sits among the crowd
listening to the strings sing.

Sophie takes lessons from Jaz now.
She even has a new guitar
that rocks a cool vintage strap.

I clench my fist,
kick at the gravel,
and race for home.

Sophie and Jaz
were strangers a month ago.
Now they're always together.

Lately, I've been wondering,
where does that leave me?

The Bad Thing About Running

The bad thing about running to clear your head is it doesn't matter how long you run, or how fast you get there, when you stop, your problems always have time to catch up

Home is Where the Silence is

Tick-tock,
Tick-tock,
goes the clock.

The house is too quiet.
No conversation.
No laughter.

Just *Pass the salt, please.*
and *Did you do your homework?*

With our noses
buried in our books,
I peek at Mom from across the room.

There are hundreds of pages
with thousands of words
to choose from,
yet none of them,

not one,

leave our lips.

Blood

-type

In my family,
there are two blood types,
B-Perfect and O-My-God.

-line

Mom comes from a long line
of type B-Perfect women.
All beautiful,
with orderly homes
and perfect lives—
at least on the surface.

-stain

Taught to hide their true feelings,
the women keep quiet,
believing imperfection
equals weakness
and weakness
tarnishes the family name.

-pressure

I know the rules,
smile no matter how you feel
and hide every bad thing.
Sometimes I feel obligated
to follow the rules, after all,
they've been passed down
for generations.

-stream
But the other blood type,
the O-My-God type,
is pumping through my veins.
It flows warm
and rebellious,
causing an openness that's
upsetting to my family.
Even scandalous.

-letting
I am a firm believer in the broken
who bandage their hurt
with the help of others.
I believe it's okay
not to be okay,
and that we should always
be ourselves
and live our truth.

-red
I refuse to be quiet.
I have made up a new rule—
no more biting tongues
until they bleed.

Chemical Bases

There are four
chemical bases
that make up all DNA.

Without them, we are nothing.

The bases sound exotic to me,
like the names
of four strong,
beautiful,
women.

Adenine,
Cytosine,
Thymine,
and Guanine—
goddesses or warriors
from a fairy tale.

Each time
the bases line up
in a different order,
they have a different
DNA story to tell.

It makes me want to find
the missing pages
of my story.

I want to read
my bio-dad's story too.

I wonder if his story
includes a chapter
on children.

I've always wanted a sister.

Unshelved

The good news is it's Friday
and I have a date with Charlie.

The bad news is it's Friday,
and I have to work first.

My cart squeaks
from section to section
as I put hundreds of books
back where they belong.

I pick up a book on oceanography
and think about how my life
went from calm seas
to hurricane
in a matter of weeks.

Like the books on my cart,
my life is out of order.
Even worse,
book one of my series
is missing.

It's like some irresponsible loser
checked it out from the library
and forgot to return it.

I wonder what the fine is
for sixteen years past due.

Date Night

Charlie asked me over
for dinner tonight.

The invitation came
with a stipulation.

No DNA talk.

I don't like stipulations,
they're like ultimatums,
only nicer.

Besides,
I don't talk about DNA that much.

Do I?

I clock out,
grab my backpack
and head for the restroom.

A quick change
into a flowy boho skirt and sandals,
and I'm out the door.

Charlie's pink clapboard cottage
is five blocks from the library
and just steps from the ocean.

The smell of an odd mixture
of dust,
saltwater,
and gasoline
hits me as I enter his garage.

Charlie is standing next to his car—
his newly painted,
orange as the sunset Mustang.

Surprise! he says,
with a sweep of his arm
as if he's the host of a game show.

I take a step closer,
I've never seen anything so beautiful!

Charlie's smile grows.
Me neither, he says,
raising his eyebrows.

Only he isn't looking at the car.

Fleeing

Dinner at Charlie's house
is like a history lesson.

The paneled walls are covered
with framed pictures
of a difficult past.

Charlie's adoptive parents
were driven from Vietnam
by war and conflict.

They fled a year apart
but their stories are the same.
Crowded, makeshift boats,
belly gnawing hunger,
raging storms,
pirates,
and disease.

They faced life
in America head-on,
with more hard work
and determination
than money or good luck.

Years later,
they found each other
and married beneath a canopy of joy.

The new bride was desperate
to become a mother,
but her womb rejected the thought.

Then Charlie fled
to the safety of her arms.

Okay, so I Broke the Rule

I may have accidentally-on-purpose
brought up the subject
of my DNA.
It's on my mind 24/7,
what does Charlie expect?
He totally overreacted!
It's not like I broke the law
or anything.

I guess he was serious,
the car ride home
was unbearably silent.
And this was the first date

ever

that didn't end with a kiss.

Lies and Cookies

I come home to the smell
of warm butter
and cinnamon.

Mom is in the kitchen
baking cookies.
She tells me she can't sleep.

Join the club, I say.

She lifts a silver platter,
piled high with
snickerdoodles.

I look at the cookies
and think about all the lies
Mom served to me with a smile.

I ate them up,
everyone,
and washed them down
with a tall glass of milk.

I shove the platter back at her.
I don't want your cookies, I snap.
I want my father's name!

Lost in Translation

When **Mom** said
she never meant to **hurt** me,

she was really saying
she never meant for me
to learn the truth

because what I don't know
can't hurt **me**.

Heart to Heart

It has been   a long time
since I have had   a talk with Dad.
When he first died,   I used to hold his
urn on my lap, whispering my plans and
secrets. Sophie once asked me if I'd ever
committed a crime. I said no, but I'd
steal my dad back from death in
a minute. I settle into his
chair for a heart to
heart. I talk, he
listens.

Hello, Dad, Are You There?

Remember the time
I was jumping rope
in your studio?
I knocked over
those candlestick holders
you were making
for a customer.
You didn't get too mad,
you just held the dustpan
while I swept up
the pieces.
I wish
you were here now
to hold the dustpan.
I have a real mess on my hands.

A Sign from Heaven

I wonder if my dad
can see me from heaven.
Is he watching my life unfold
like our origami crane?
He must know
I can't trace the creases
and refold it this time.

I wonder if he's sad
because I want to find
my bio-dad.

I tell him it doesn't mean
I love him any less.

Let me know if it's okay, I whisper.
Give me a sign!

I Give Up

After a while with no sign
I return Dad's urn
to the mantle
and curl up
like a question mark
for a nap in his chair.

I push in my earbuds
and listen
to Michael Bublé sing about
it all working out someday.

My eyelids
are beginning to droop
when my phone chimes.

I look at the message
from my-dna.org.

You have a new DNA relative.
connect with them now!

Better Late than Never

Click.
Sign in.
Search.

A new relative shows up
in my *family connections*.
It's not my bio-dad.
Not even close.
Still, the email came
right after I asked my dad
to give me a sign,
to let me know
if he's okay
with my search
for Bio-dad.

The message said
connect with them now.

could this be the sign?

How to Find a Bio-Dad in Five Steps

1.
Open your mind to possibilities.
Open your laptop.
Listen as it hums to life.

2.
Perform magic.
Using photo editing software,
make your mom disappear from the ski photo.

3.
Grasp at straws.
Send an email to all distant relatives.
Subject line: Do you know this man?

4.
Ask for help.
Lower yourself to the floor.
Bow your head and pray.

5.
Repeat step four.
Pray again, harder this time.
Bargain with God if you have to.

One Track Mind

All my talk about DNA
is wearing on Charlie
like sand trapped in his shoes.

Tonight, he wants to talk.

He says my paternity
is all I talk about anymore,
the only thing I think about.

He confesses his heart breaks
a little bit more every time I say
I don't know who I am.

Charlie is not related by blood
to anyone in his family.
He asks me if that makes him
less of a son,
a nephew,
a cousin,
if it makes his mom and dad
lesser parents.

Then it happens.
The words roll off my tongue
before checking with my brain.

It's different, I say,
my biological father might want me.

Charlie takes a step back,
dodging the invisible punch.

It's over between us, Aspen, he says.
We are two different people.

And I don't need a DNA test to tell me that.

No Tomorrow

I burst out the door
and take off running
like there's no tomorrow.

Because for Charlie and me,
I don't think there is.

Breaking (Up) News

Live at 10 pm.
Charlie calls it quits!

I can't blame him.
I'm broken.
I admit it.

I wish Charlie could still love me.
All of me.
Even the jagged pieces.

When I share the news,
Sophie and Jaz say it's his loss.
Jaxon says Charlie's a fool for letting me go.
Auntie Allison mails chocolate.
I don't tell Mom. She doesn't ask.

I don't need you.
You don't deserve me.
I never loved you anyway.

Lies I Tell Myself

Bedtime Story

Lying in bed
looking at the picture of Mom and Luke,
I'm reminded of a story
Mom told me once:

> *The snowfall was breathtaking,*
> *blanketing pines in thick,*
> *downy comforters.*
> *Then came the blizzard!*
> *We were trapped*
> *inside a rustic cabin.*
> *We snuggled*
> *until the roads cleared.*
> *You were conceived in love.*

I look at the date on the picture,
February 2nd.

My birthday is on November 8th,
a little over nine months
after Mom's ski trip.

When Mom shared her story,
she forgot to share
the most important part.

Dad wasn't even there.

The Color of Lies

I've told a mountain
of white lies in my life,
tall enough to ski down.
But I draw the line there,
in the fresh powder.
Because the darker lies,
the deep purple ones,
those lies hurt
like a bruise,
and leave scars
that sometimes never fade.

Clue #2

Goodbye is never final
in a small town.

How can I learn to unlove Charlie
when I see him everywhere I go,
when I feel him in everything I do?

I choose Hype Café
over Java Junkie,
but my pumpkin spice latte
still tastes like Charlie's kiss.

Sitting at a table in the back,
I stare at the picture
of Mom and Luke.

I ZOOM in,
scanning Luke's face,
searching for similarities to mine.

That's when I notice
the logo on Luke's jacket.
A fold in the material
makes the embroidered letters hard to read.

I wish I could crawl
inside the photo
and learn where they are.
I'd smack that grin
off Mom's face while I was at it.

When I look closer,
I can make out four letters—*rock*.

I Google the words
ski resort + rock
and get a hit on a website:

Discover the beautiful
Snow Rock Ski Resort
in Aspen, Colorado!

A chill of understanding
shoots through me.

Aspen, Colorado.
Aspen Deluca.

I close my eyes.
This is where I began.

I Text Sophie

Call me!

Sophie replies with a picture
of her and Jaz on horseback,
smiling under the shade
of identical cowboy hats.

@ family reunion in Texas, Call u later.

Sophie is Ghosting Me

I feel a cold draft
where our friendship
used to be.

Pleading

I know I shouldn't do it.
But I'm desperate.
I call Charlie
for a ride to Colorado.

If I can get there,
I can ask around,
show the picture.

Maybe somebody remembers Luke.
Or knows him.

Charlie answers his phone.
What do you want, Aspen?
We broke up, remember?

I beg him to take me.
Please!

He says he can't drop everything
for a wild goose chase.

But I need this, Charlie,
I don't know where I'm from! I cry.

Charlie says he doesn't know
his biological parents,
yet he knows exactly where he's from.

He's from nighttime baths
and goodnight kisses,
from little league games
and family picnics,
and from miracles
that lead him
to a better life.

Reach beyond your genes, Aspen, he says.
When you figure out where you're from, let me know.

He hangs up.

Lurker

I don't know how it started
but it did.

I've been spying on Charlie.
Logging on to social media,
sneaking a peek at his posts,
his pictures,
his comments.
Lurking like a stalker.
Today Charlie blocked me
and changed his status to
"Single."

I don't know how it ended
but it did.

Smooth(ie) Move

In desperate need of a story
to whisk me far away
from the adventures of Aspen
and her sorry-ass life,
I rummage through my hoard of books.

I'm just settling in to read
when I get a text from Jaxon Lee.

RESCUE ME!

He's training for a relay race
and needs someone to pace him.

I don't feel like running
on a track in circles
like a hamster on a wheel,
but he lures me there
with the promise of a smoothie.

We're just running partners.
Nothing more.

Yet as I tie my shoes
I can't help but smile.

Monday Lunch Bell

When the bell rings,
I ping-pong
down the crowded hall
making my way to the cafeteria.

With Jaz and Sophie
at their family reunion,
our usual table sits empty.

When I spot Charlie,
he looks the other way,
pretending not to see me.

Evie and Riley wave,
inviting me to sit.
We're old teammates
from swim camp.
I swam butterfly,
they killed it in breaststroke.

I wave back,
but I don't sit down.
I don't feel like talking.

Besides, I'm not hungry.
I've filled up on sadness
and left no room for dessert.

I push through
the cafeteria doors,
and take the steps
                down

                    to

                        the

                            one

                                place

I never feel alone.

Lunch in the Library

This is my refuge,
my cozy den,
where characters live
and welcome me in.
It's my well
and my garden,
the place where I go
to quench my thirst
and feed my soul.

Writer's Block

A sheet
of notebook paper
lies on my desk.

With pen in hand,
I look out my window
at the crisp fall morning.

Snails scribble messages
in iridescent ink
on stone pavers.

A flock of scrub jays
line up like a sentence
on the fence rail.

A woodpecker
types out a poem
with its beak on birch.

If only words
came to me as easily.

I start to write.
I stop.

Start
Stop
Start
Stop

Crumbled paper
surrounds me like confetti
by the time I find my words.

Dear Charlie

Where I'm From.

I am from sandcastles,
from sea glass and lemonade stands.
I am from a windy November morning
dreaming of spring.
I am from swollen bee stings
and get-better kisses medicated with love.

I'm from big hugs and freckles,
from Cecelia and Grandpa Pepper.
I'm from *Mind your manners*
and *You can do anything you set your mind to*,
from never giving up and never giving in.

I'm from burning lungs and shin splints.
I'm from the gulls and the sea, cannoli, and calzones.
From the tire swing Dad hung from the old oak tree,
the sunshine song Mom sang that still plays in my
head.

On my dresser is a stack of novels
waiting to be re-read.
I am from those books,
from characters with strong spines
and words captured like butterflies from their pages.

Sorry Looking Equation

I try to do homework
but give up on geometry
the minute I open the book.

How can I solve
math problems for school
when all I can think about
is my sorry-looking equation.

Me
Minus Dad
Minus Mom
Minus Charlie
Minus Sophie

1 - 4 = My life sucks.

Pain Management

With my homework forgotten,
I head out the door.

The
pound
pound
pounding
of my feet
on pavement
is just what I need.

I take a deep,
calming breath
of October's perfume—
A fragrant mix
of pine needles,
squishy plums,
and smoke from cozy fireplaces.

When I reach town,
I stop to stretch my legs
and check my phone.

There are no messages,
except for the stash
of old texts from Charlie.
The ones my heart
won't let me delete.

Good morning sexy!
See you soon
Sweet dreams babe

Mr. Gray's garden
is buzzing with an array
of bright colors.

His orange Calla Lilies
have faded with summer,
making room for fall blossoms.

I reach over the fence
and snatch a pink Dahlia.

Plucking petals
one by one,
I repeat an old chant.

He loves me.
He loves me not.

But the words change
when you get older
and do something stupid.

Loves Me Loves Me Not

Word Problem

You just ran 10 miles to ease the pain of missing your ex-boyfriend when you see 3 friends who tell you they saw Charlie at the park 30 minutes ago. So, you run an additional 2.5 miles hoping to talk to him, maybe work things out. When you reach the park, you find Charlie playing frisbee with 1 flirty girl named Violet from the coffee shop where they work. Seeing them together breaks your heart into a million pieces. What do you have left?

The Last Petal

He loves me not.

Unboxing Answers

It's hanging in the kitchen.
The key to possible answers.

When Mom walks out the door,
I lunge for it.

How did I forget
about the locked shed
and the answers it could be holding?

I am being raised a Deluca
but I am something else too—
I need to know
what that something else is.

Minutes later, a box marked,
YEARBOOKS
sits on my bedroom floor
shedding dust like dandruff.

Maybe Mom met Luke in college.
Maybe they hooked up later.

My bio-dad could be hiding
between the covers
of these old books,
just waiting to be found.

I burn a pan of brownies,
crack open the window,
and settle in for a night
of serious searching.

Mom's Yearbooks

The box holds
> Mom's college yearbooks
> from freshman to senior year.

The books hold
> hundreds of pages
> with thousands
> of tiny square pictures.

The margins hold
> names in alphabetical order.
> Last names are of no use to me.

The back pages hold
> Doodles
> and dorky messages to Mom—
> none of them are from a guy named Luke.

Blizzard

By the time I reach the last page,
of the last yearbook,
I've found
eight Lukes,
five Lucases
and one Luca.

Possible fathers.

I work the list
like a logic puzzle,
crossing off names
until I am down to just one—

Lucas M. Alanis.

He's Greek.
He has dimples.
Alanis is a surname listed on my DNA website.
He was a football player.
Mom was a cheerleader.

I fall asleep
with the window open,
a blizzard of yearbooks on my bed
but I'm warm with the hope
of finding my biological father.

Finally!

A New Day

I wake to Mom standing over me,
already dressed for the day,
picture perfect, as always—
except for the scowl on her face.
What are you doing with my yearbooks?

Looking for my bio-dad, I yawn.

You won't find anything here, she says.
Honestly, Aspen, let it go!

I return the books to Mom.
I don't need them anymore.
I have what I need,
my bio-dad's name.

Did you love him? I ask.

It doesn't matter, she says.
*He had a wife
and I had a husband.*

Mom hovers in the doorway,
*Dad adored you, Aspen.
Why isn't that enough?*

Before I can answer,
she turns and stomps away,
clutching the box of yearbooks
to her cold heart.

I pause to swipe at a tear
then close and lock my door.

It's easy for people
who know who they are
to say stuff like that.

But I'll tell you right now,
when the blood inside a stranger
is inside you,
you want to know who he is.

When She Sees Me

When Mom looks at me,
is it his face she sees?
The brown eyes?
The curls?
The dimples?

When Mom tells me
she thinks I'm special,
is it because I am me?
Or because I am from him?

When she calls my name,
does she think of her ski trip?
The snow?
The cabin?

When she looks at me
day after day,
year
after
year,
and quietly protects
her secret.

Has she ever once thought,
The girl has a right to know?

The Call

With shaky hands,
I dial the number I found online
for Lucas M. Alanis.
I literally have my future
in the palm of my hand.

After a brief hold,
a man with a thick accent answers.

Is this Lucas Alanis? I ask.

He's silent for a second,
This is Father Alanis. How may I help you?

F-F-ather? I stammer.

Yes, he says,
of St. Christopher's Parish.
What can I do for you, child?

First, I panic.
Then I hang up.

Crap!
Wrong kind of father.

Spam

I've been praying
a lot lately.
I leave long,
sobbing messages
asking God
to help Mom
understand how I feel.
For her to tell me
the truth
about my biological father.
But my messages
go unanswered.
I wonder if He's unhappy
with something I did.
Or didn't do.
I have a bad feeling
God is blocking my calls.

Observation

There are
twenty three
pairs of
chromosomes in
the
human
body. It has
been twenty
three days
since Charlie
split. Twenty
three days
of conversation
lost. Twenty
three days
of unsent
texts. Twenty
three days
of missed
kisses.
Twenty
three days
of regret

Second Place Friend

Finally, a text from Sophie!

Jaz is practicing for a concert,
so Sophie has some free time.
She wants to hang out.

I miss Sophie
but what I hear is,
I'd rather be with my cousin.
You're in second place.
I'm super busy with my new life,
busy
busy
busy.

My thumbs hover over the keypad.

I miss my best friend.
I want to hang out.
Maybe go to a movie.
Bowling.
But not like this.

I type my answer.

I'm busy.

Checking Me Out

Jaxon came by
the library tonight
to "check out some books."

He stayed for a long time,
glancing my way
as he pulled book after book
off the shelves.

Stephen King.
Patricia Cornwell.
James Patterson.

Mysteries.

While he looked.
I looked too.

He'd replaced his running gear
with black jeans and boots,
his dark hair freed
from its ponytail.

As he handed the books
over the counter
his fingers touched mine.

I wondered if he could
feel my skin tingle,
hear my heart

POUND.

Hey beautiful, he library-whispered.
I'm throwing a Halloween party tonight.
You should come.

I was tempted,
man, was I tempted,
but I told him no.

The last thing I want to do
is dress up and pretend
to be somebody I'm not.

Been there.
Doing that.

Sugar Low

Halloween is the beginning
of All Hallowtide,
a time to remember the dead.

I don't need a special day.
I think of my dad all the time.

Vampire Mom went to a party
leaving a bowl of candy
for me to divvy out
to trick-or-treaters.

I turn out the lights instead
and binge on horror movies
and Hershey bars.

Poison Oak

At ten o'clock
ghosts and goblins
have long given up
their march for sweets.

I sink into the faded
Adirondack chair
in the front courtyard.

Mom's garden gloves
lie on the ground
crusted with mud,
still clinging
to memories
of spring poppies.

I catch my reflection in the window.

Who is that sad, angry girl?

Mom planted hurt
inside my heart.

I tended it with anger
and watered it
with resentment.

Now the prickly vine
has taken over
and it's choking out

all
the
pretty
flowers.

Dork

I'm playing fetch with Nova
when I get a text message.

Jaxon sent a picture of trees.
I thought of u 2 day.

I text back,
u think of me when u c trees?

He replies,
only the Aspens.

Dorky.
But Sweet.

I send a picture of us at the lighthouse.
thought of u 2 day 2.

Seconds later.
wanna run?

Butterflies

The butterfly sanctuary
is open when we run by
so Jaxon and I go inside.

Hundreds of the insects
swirl around our heads,
their amber wings
like tiny stained-glass windows.

When they land on my arm
I notice their elaborate
white markings.
It's as if a painter
dipped and dotted
her way
through thousands
of paper wings.

Jaxon's taking a video,
trying to capture their dance.

I envy them, I say.

Yeah, Jaxon agrees.
Why run when you can fly?

At the top of the trees,
clusters of butterflies hang,
dripping
from branches
like old leaves.

I turn to take a picture
and collide with Jaxon.

He grabs hold of me
so I don't fall.
Careful, he winks.

Suddenly, I feel warm
and tingly all over.

And I wonder…
is this a date?

Rough Night

Mom and I fought.
Again.

For a smart woman,
she says stupid things.

I was moving
her sewing machine
into the dining room for her
when she tried to convince me
that DNA is overrated,
that it's not genes
but our souls
that make us who we are.

She said I look nothing like Luke.
Act nothing like him.

She might as well have stabbed me
with the seam ripper
she was holding.

I get it.
She's working overtime
on damage control
but I'm not buying it.

My mannerisms,
personality,
likes,
and dislikes
are more connected
to my genetics
than she realizes.

Whether she wants
to admit it
or not,
my bio-dad's genes
are sewn into the fabric
of who I am.

Call me stubborn,
but as much as I love Dad,
I can't pretend
the Deluca genes fit me.

They never have.

Sorry Not Sorry

I'm in my room
when Mom shuffles in
clutching a box of tissues.

Her blue eyes
are puffy and swollen,
my brown eyes
are tired and bloodshot.

Today we look alike
for the first time
in our lives.

She sits on the edge of my bed,
When I learned I was pregnant
with another man's child,
I chose to stay with my husband.

Mom pauses to take my hand,
It was in your best interest.
We had Cooper.
We were a family.

Come on, I say, pulling my hand free of her grip.
It was in your best interest, Mom.
Think about it. Lying made your life easier.

No finger-pointing
No shame
No messy divorce

Mom shakes her head,
You're wrong; I did it for you.

Gee, thanks. I roll my eyes.
I've always wanted to live a lie; how did you know?

Last year if someone told me
Mom was keeping a secret like this,
I would have said they were
a few fries short of a Happy Meal.

I'm not sure who she is anymore.
She pretends to be so proper.

She's the one who taught me
that the easy way
and the right way
are two entirely different things.

Mom lifts her chin,
Would you rather I didn't have you?

Apparently, in her mind
lying to Dad and abortion
were her only choices.

I would have rather you told me the truth. I sigh.
*I would have rather grown up knowing I had two dads—
whether they were in my life or not.*

Mom stands and walks to the door.
I'm sorry you feel that way.

I look down at my snotty tissue
and try again,

Who is he, Mom?

When I look up.
She's gone.

Crumbs

As far as apologies go,
"I'm sorry you feel that way," isn't one.

I wanted to hear Mom say
she was wrong.

> Wrong to define my life
> with her lie.

> Wrong to force me
> to live her secret.

> Wrong to deliberately
> take away my choice.

I wanted her to save
our relationship,
to make us right again.

I wanted to hear
my father's name
tumble from her lips

Instead, I got
"I'm sorry you feel that way."

And you know what?
I'll take it.

Mom's throwing crumbs
and I'm hungry.

Mixed Feelings

I'm soaking
in a tub of bubbles
when I get a text from Sophie.

I miss hanging with you!

In the picture she sent,
we're six years old
hanging upside down
on a jungle gym
like chimpanzees.

Wild hair.
Wide smiles.

I can see the bandage
on my leg from a fall
into the gravel below.

Little Sophie raced home
for first aid supplies
then pronounced me "all better"
in her best doctor's voice.

In her text,
she says she's been
a crappy friend lately.

I have to agree.

She wants to make it up to me.

How about a spa night?
Just us.
My house 7:00?

I hesitate.

Aspen?

I look at the picture again,
the grins on our
up-side-down faces.

I miss hanging with Sophie too.
I shoot a text back.

I'll bring take-out!

Spa Night

With our fingernails
painted black
and our faces
smeared with goo
that's guaranteed
to make us gorgeous,
we snap selfies,
giggling
like best friends do.

I'm posting this! Sophie laughs.

I tell Sophie I've missed this.
Things changed a lot between us
when she found Jaz.

I've been a butthead. Sophie frowns.
I was just excited to find a relative.
I'm sorry for ignoring you.

A lifetime of friendship
flashes through my mind.
Road trips
Concerts
Pranks

I throw a pillow at her head.
I forgive you, I laugh.

She posts our picture.
#spaday
#chill
#friendsforlife

I may have a new cousin, she smiles,
but you'll always be my ketchup sister.

Mission Impossible

I call Sophie on Saturday
and she agrees to join me
on a clue-finding mission.

She hugs me, *Sorry, I'm late,*
I had to repair my car.
Her side mirror
is strapped in place
with neon duct tape.

Nice! I laugh.

We climb in
for the short drive
across town.

I lean back
in the vintage VW seat
and close my eyes.

I try to hide it
but Sophie knows
what I'm thinking.

She gave up boys
like a bad habit last year
after a harsh breakup.

Charlie will come around, she says.
Just give him time.

I open my eyes
as we pass Java Junkie
and see Charlie through the window,
laughing with Violet.

Sighing, I turn to Sophie,
I think I've run out of time.

Strip Search

Every newspaper
printed in our town
is stored at the library
on reels of microfilm.

Sophie and I sit side by side
at the microfilm reader,
zooming in,
spinning the dial,
focusing on headlines.

There are thousands
of articles,
documents,
and journals
to look through.

I find my birth announcement
along with a picture.
I'm swaddled
in a striped blanket—
a little alien with round eyes.

Peter and Cecelia Deluca
welcomed a baby girl,
Aspen Marie Deluca,
on November 8th.
6 lbs., 7 oz. 20 inches long.

We keep up the search
until Mrs. Dunn closes
the library for the night.

Disappointed,
we grab our backpacks
and head for the door.

Another dead end.

Criminal

Still in detective mode,
Sophie informs me
that what my mom did was illegal.

What are you talking about? I say.

It's true, Aspen. I Googled it!

Sophie says it's against the law
to purposely claim the wrong man
as the father of your child
on a birth certificate—a legal document.

It's called paternity fraud, Sophie adds.
She could go to jail.

I'm glad I'm not the only one
who thinks what my mom did
is all kinds of wrong.

Does your mom like wearing jumpsuits? Sophie smiles.

I laugh, *not really, but orange is her favorite color.*

REAL-izing

I'm sitting on the floor,
back propped against
my unmade bed,
dad-keepsakes
on my lap.

I've been thinking
a lot lately about
what makes a dad,
a dad.

Is it genetics?
Or is it something else?

I look at the faded pictures,
read the hand-written cards,
examine each trinket.

Images of deep-sea fishing,
boogie boarding,
and playing video games
circle in my brain
like reruns of favorite movies.

Dad was at the hospital
when I was born.

He stuck up for me
and stuck by me,
no matter what.

When I was little,
he came to my tea parties—
and never said *no* to a frilly hat.

The memories warm me.
I close my eyes,
and I know…

Dad was my REAL dad.

My bio-dad?
He's a bonus.

Running Into Jaxon

I saw you on the side of the road,
shirt clinging to your body

in

the   rain

You had been trying
to outrun the storm,
like I had been.

Me in my running shoes,
you in your jacked-up Jeep,
top down.

In a zip and a snap,
we were cruising down
the road, heat cranked.

My mind raced.
Did yours?

You pulled up
to the drive-through
for burgers with a side of awkward.

While you ordered,
I chewed on my cuticles,
a tasteless appetizer.

My stomach did flip-flops.
        Did yours?

When I asked you
to drop me off at the store,
you said, "Anything your heart desires."

Parked at the curb,
you opened my door
and leaned in.

I lifted my chin,
waited...

A horn blared,
interrupting the moment
so, we said goodbye
and you drove away.

You said, "anything your heart desires."

        My heart desired a kiss.
        Did yours?

Understanding

My all-time favorite book
is *To Kill a Mockingbird*.
Atticus Finch taught me
that you really never understand a person
until you've considered things
from their point of view.
He said you have to
"Climb into his skin and walk around in it."

I hate to admit it
but I think I understand
how Mom could have had feelings
for two guys at the same time.

To the Lady at the Store Looking at DNA Tests

It is a new world.
Anyone
can learn their DNA story.

Deciphering
our secret code is exciting,
the key to genetic insight,
information,
and opportunity.

Some people shy away
from science,
others embrace it.

Once a decision
is made to commit,
hold on!

A genetic journey
lies
in each drop of spit.

Results can change lives,
better understand,
it's real.

Naked

I wake at midnight
to Charlie calling my name.

He's beneath my window,
denim shirt billowing
in the breeze.

We run barefoot to the beach.

He kisses me long
and slow,
pulls my nightgown over my head,
covers my body with his.

We swirl together like taffy,
sweet and salty,
beneath a blue moon.

I close my eyes
as warm hands explore my body.

When I peek through my lashes,
Charlie is grinning.
But his sea-green eyes
have turned brown
and his beautiful blonde curls
have morphed into dark waves.

Suddenly it's Jaxon!
And I'm lying naked in his arms.

I wake with a jolt.
Sweating.
Heart pounding.
Tangled in my sheets.

Alone.
And missing Charlie.

Wake Up Call

Sometimes a dream wakes you
like thunder in the night.
And when it does,
you know exactly what you want.

4 Reasons Charlie is the 1

1. The smirk that lurks beneath his grin.
2. His heart, the part that drew me in.
3. His kiss I miss upon my face.
4. The thrill I feel in his embrace.

Fat Favor

I head to Jaz' house at an easy jog,
still yawning
from a sleepless night.

When she opens the door
she's shocked to see me.

I get it.
We aren't exactly friends.

She steps back,
inviting me inside.
Her house reminds me
of our local music store,
guitars,
keyboards,
and drums
filling every corner.

Jaz inherited her musical ability
from her mom.

What's up? she asks,
offering me a seat
on a narrow piano bench.

I tell her my idea,
the one where she helps me
write a song for Charlie.

I suppose you'll want me to sing it too, she says.

I nod.

If Jaz doesn't agree to help,
I don't know if I'll ever
get Charlie back.

Even then, it's a crapshoot.

I was an insensitive jerk.
Charlie's adoptive mom and dad
are his real parents,
just like Peter was my real dad.
I understand that now.

I look at Jaz, hopefully.
Sure, she smiles,
I'm a sucker for a love song.

We make plans to meet up tomorrow.

Right now, there is one more thing
I need to do.

Words

I text Jaxon
asking him to meet me
at the trail gate.

When he shows up,
I gather my words.

Words in my head
I've been practicing
over and over.

Words in my mouth
like a too-hot mint
I'm dying to spit out.

Flirting
Confused
Feelings
Mistake
I can't do this
I Love Charlie

Jaxon shares words too,
surprising words,

Just friends
Not my type
Sorry
Wrong impression
Involved with someone else

When I turn to leave,
Jaxon gently grabs my arm,
Wait! Aren't we running?

I shake my head,
Not today.

I came here
to break it off with Jaxon.

So why am I the one
who feels rejected?

Songwriting Session

The next day after school
Sophie and I meet Jaz
at her locker.

She grabs her old,
scuffed-up guitar case
and we head to her house.

Jaz's tiny room is plastered
with music posters
on the walls,
on the ceiling,
all around us,
rock,
rap,
pop,
country too.

Jaz hands me a notebook and a pen.
I can write a twelve-page essay
with my eyes closed
but a song?

Out of my element.

It's simple, Jaz says,
poetry comes from the heart
and a song is like a poem set to music.

Simple for you, Jaz! Sophie laughs.

I know what my heart
wants to say to Charlie
so, I start there.

It's late when we leave.
But I'm happy.

Charlie has a song.
We have a plan.

Jaz will sing the song
on stage at Hype Café
tomorrow night.

Sophie is in charge
of getting Charlie there.

Performance Night

A hum of excitement
fills the night air.

I peek out
from my hiding spot
behind a hibiscus draped trellis.

Twinkling party lights
are strung crisscrossed
over the small outside patio.

Jaz is on stage, setting up.
Test
Test

I spot Sophie leading Charlie
to a table in front.

She begged Charlie
to be her date tonight,
said she didn't want to go alone.

He only agreed
when she told him
I was in New York visiting Cooper.

Another lie.

It isn't long before Jaz
is jamming on her guitar.
Upbeat songs
followed by
beautiful ballads.

The night is getting colder
but I welcome its breath
on my too-warm cheeks.

When Jaz has sung
what seems to be her last song,
she speaks into the microphone.

This is it.
I hold my breath.

Watching.
Waiting.

A few days ago, a friend came to me, asking for help.
She wanted to do something special for someone special.

Charlie, this song is for you...

Charlies Song ♪

If I'm sorry was a song, this is how it would sound.
Like a needle on vinyl, we've gone round and round.
My world has gone crazy. I don't know what's true
except that I'm crazy in love with you.

Forgive Me and Apology would play a duet.
The rhythm would rock the stage with regret.
I know you are hurting, and I am to blame.
If I'm sorry was a song, I'd sing it all day.

I can't unsay words or unbreak your heart,
but you and me, baby, we can make a new start.
Melody and lyrics can't right all the wrongs,
but baby, just listen before moving on.

Forgive Me and Apology would play a duet.
The rhythm would rock the stage with regret.
I know you are hurting, and I am to blame.
If I'm sorry was a song, I'd sing it all day.

Sing it all day.
Sing it all day.

The Crowd Goes Wild

Charlie's song ends
to rousing applause.

He twists in his seat,
looking for me—
or for the exit,
I'm not sure.

I step from my hiding place,
turning to face him.

Warm, green eyes,
a wild mop of blond hair,
worn jeans that fit him just right.

God, he's gorgeous.

He stands up,
smiles,
stretches his arms
out to his side
like the wings of a bird in flight.

My heart soars.

I run to him
and leap into his arms.
He spins me around
while the crowd cheers us on.

His embrace feels
a little like forgiveness
and a lot like coming home.

When Charlie releases me,
my feet touch the ground.

But I'm floating.

I look over at Sophie and Jaz
wearing identical smiles
and give them a wave of thanks.

Charlie takes my hand,
presses it to his heart,
Come on, he whispers, *let's get out of here.*

xoxo

And there we are
back in Charlie's Mustang
like nothing ever happened.

Only it did.

Before Charlie has a chance
to say one word
I tell him again how sorry I am.
We have different views
but that doesn't mean
we can't get along.

He says he's sorry too,
that he could have been
more understanding.

We are like tightrope walkers
trying to find our balance
in a strong wind.
Only now, the blindfold is off.

When Charlie kisses me
I find myself thinking,
that make-up kisses make breakups
almost worth it.

Auntie Allison

My Auntie called today
to wish me an early
Happy Birthday.

She said the older I get
the more I remind her
of my dad, her brother.

She still gets the urge
to pick up her phone
and call him,
then she remembers he's gone.

But she says she takes comfort
in knowing Dad lives on
through me.

I am such a fraud.

Dear DNA

I still don't know
how to pronounce your name.
Forgive me for using your initials.

What you revealed shattered my world,
but I want you to know
I'm not mad at you for telling.

If I blamed you,
I'd also have to blame the cells
that take instruction from you.

My genes would be in trouble too.

Nope, the way I see it,
we're all in this together.

You really do suck at keeping secrets
but I'm glad you blabbed.

It hurts to think I could have gone
my whole life unaware I share you
with a father I don't know.

It hurts to think
of the lost opportunities.
Possibilities.

I don't know how things will turn out
with my biological father,
but I want you to know
there are no hard feelings.

Yours truly,
Aspen

P.S. Thanks for the dimples.

Happy Birthday to Me

I wake up at
7:32 a.m.thinking one
thing,16 years,4 hours, 22
minutes and 7 seconds is a
long time to live my life as a
secret. I roll out of bed and I
hit the shower. Charlie and
Sophie are picking me up
in an hour. I don't know
where they are taking
me and my sneaky
friends aren't
talk-
ing.

I'm not sure I can handle another surprise.

Road Trip

I'm sitting
next to Charlie
in the front seat of his car.

Sophie rides in back,
her long legs
stretched
across worn leather seats.

We speed three miles
down the California highway
before I figure out where we're going.

To the beach boardwalk!

I roll down my window
and breathe in the salty air.

Sophie tugs on her earbuds,
cranks up her music
and we sing out loud.

I smile, Charlie knows
all the wrong words
to my favorite song.

Promises

A tsunami
of rollercoaster screams hits us
as we pull into the parking lot.

Charlie slides
his Mustang into a spot
next to railroad tracks long forgotten.

We follow a cotton candy breeze
through a maze of cars
to the entrance
of the oceanside park.

As we climb the steps
to Funtime Town,
Charlie whispers,
Promise me something?

That depends. I say.

Don't worry today, he says.
Just. Have. Fun.

He slips his hand in mine
so we can shake on it.

I tighten my grip
and pull him in
for a kiss to seal the deal.

Zap

At laser tag,
we're paired up with three dudes.
We grab our gear and suit up.

I scope things out
before the door closes us
in darkness.

Putting my back against the wall,
I aim at the moving
electronic targets.

ZAP

                         ZAP

      ZAP

With fast fingers,
I knock out a few points
right off the bat.

It feels good to let out my frustration.

ZAP Cancer

ZAP Lies

ZAP Secrets

We hide,
dodge,
and dive
through obstacles
of props and barricades,

looking for shadow,
for movement,
for light.

ZAP

I'm on fire!

A player's phaser locks up
leaving him unprotected.

Game over.

We push through the exit doors,

bodies bumping,
hearts jumping,
fists pumping.

For the first time
in a long time,

I laugh.

Zorba

A mechanical psychic
lures me to her booth
with glowing eyes and exotic dress.

Zorba knows all, she says
with a mysterious accent.

I feed four tokens into the machine.
My vibes shoot
through the metal handle.
I grip it tighter.
Ask my question.

Will I ever find my biological father?

Sophie smiles at me, and we wait.

Zorba's fingers dazzle
with gemstones over
a deck of cards.

She chooses a card
and drops it into the slot below.

And so it will be, she says
as her lights fade out.

I reach in
to fish out the card…

THE ANSWER IS NO

What the hell!
I thought these machines
spit out optimistic predictions.

Sophie snatches
the card from my hand
and throws it in the trash can.

Don't listen to Zorba, Aspen.
She's a hater.

Say Cheese

Thump
Bump
Whack
Smack

A photo booth
is not made to hold
three full-sized people.

We strike pose
after crazy pose
until we're out of tokens,
then spill from the booth
like clowns from a funny car.

We're waiting
for our pictures to process
when I see some familiar faces.

I try to hide
behind Charlie's broad shoulders
but I'm not quick enough.

Aspen? the man says.

It's my dad's friend, Tim.
His daughter Emma is my age.

It's hard to see them
like this, Father. Daughter.
Out having fun together.

I look at them
and find myself birthday-wishing
for my old life back.

The one where I had only one dad
and he was alive.

Party Crasher

There you are, Envy,
I've seen you
hanging around.

　　　At the pier when I was twelve
　　　by the beach cruisers
　　　I couldn't afford to buy.

　　　At school with girls in skinny jeans
　　　my not-so-skinny butt
　　　could ever shimmy into.

　　　Online in the postings
　　　of pretty faces
　　　with pretty lives.

And here you are again,
dressed in green—
your favorite color.

Dancing around dads and daughters
like you were invited
to the party.

Virtual Birthday Party

Charlie pulls to a stop
in front of my house
and I climb out.

A Sweet Sixteen banner
waves in the breeze
from the eves
of our little beach house.

The late evening sunshine
still warm and bright
reminds me of Mom.

BDT (before DNA Test),
I would have been eager
to share details of my day with Mom.
But things are different between us now.

We've perfected the art
of shallow conversation.
Our forecast is holding at gray skies
with little chance of sunshine.

The *whap* of the screen door
announces I'm home.

Happy Birthday to You!

Mom sings along with Cooper,
who's on video chat.

It's good to see my brother
and to hear his voice.

I didn't realize
how much I'd miss him
when he left for school.

I can tell by our conversation
and Mom's forced smile
that she hasn't told him the news.

I open my present —
an e-reader already charged
and loaded with books.

I'm not sure how I feel about
a book without pages
to turn,
to smell,
to dog-ear (sorry Mrs. Dunn),

but I smile, *thank you!*

I blow Cooper a kiss,
take my "book" into the living room,
and settle into Dad's recliner.

The F Word

Forgiveness is a marathon,
not quick,
never easy.

It's warming up,
taking the first step
and then another.

It's leaving anger
at the starting block,
along with bitterness.

Forgiveness is uncomfortable,
like hot sun
on exposed skin.

It's falling
and getting up again,
despite the fatigue.

I'm still running,
I see the finish line,
but I'm not there, not yet.

Clue #3

I'm getting ready
to meet my friends
at the beach when my phone chimes.

To: runninggirl@email.com
From: Kacia131@rtu.com

That picture you sent, I'd know Luke Zikas anywhere.
I haven't heard from my cousin since I moved to
Japan 18 years ago.

Kacia

Treasure

Digging deep,
Charlie, Sophie, and I
fill buckets
with cool,
wet
sand.
Building walls
and turrets
and towers.

I've been digging, I tell them.
And I've found something.

A treasure? Sophie teases.

You could say that.

I tell them I know
my bio-dad's name,
that I found his address
and telephone number online.
He lives nearby, I say.

Charlie hugs me tight.
I'm happy for you, babe.

Sophie is more enthusiastic.
She tackles me to the ground
with squeals of laughter.

Sand flies in celebration.

The Plan

Charlie asks
how I'll contact Luke.

I've had time to think about this.
I invited worry
into my room last night
and she kept me awake for hours.

If I send a letter, it could get lost.
If I call, Luke could hang up on me.

I'm going to his house, I say.

Tomorrow.

Scenarios

When I think about meeting my bio-dad,
I play a game in my head.

> He's a nice man
> with dimples just like mine.
> He hugs me and says,
> "I've always wanted a daughter."
> He opens his door to me.
> We spend the rest of our lives together.
> I win

But sometimes, the game in my head changes.

> He's a mean man
> with dimples just like mine.
> He shrugs and says,
> "You're not my daughter."
> He slams his door in my face.
> We spend the rest of our lives apart.
> I lose.

I know which game I want to play
but I have a feeling reality might be

> somewhere
> in
> the
> middle.

Good Luck Chuck

Tomorrow
Sophie will drive me
to my bio-dad's house.

Tonight
Charlie comes over
to wish me luck.

He can't join us.
He'll be touring college campuses
all day with his parents.

I'll miss having Charlie
by my side,
he makes everything better.

I pinky-promise
I'll call him with details
if I meet Bio-dad.

We hang out.
Make popcorn.
Watch a movie.

He gives me a pep talk
and I pretend I'm not scared

spitless.

Letting Go

I've been letting anger
play on a loop in my heart
like a favorite song for too long.

Maybe it's the compassion
I see in Charlie
towards his parents.

Or maybe I'm just tired
of being miserable.

But I'm ready to move on.

I know it won't be easy.
Forgiveness is a process.
I'll have to take it
step
by
step.

I creep down the hallway
clutching the note I wrote
to my chest.

When I slip it beneath Mom's door,
the breeze from her open window
tugs it from my fingertips.

Whoosh!

Dear Mom

I know you have your reasons
for not telling me I have another dad
and for not telling him he has a daughter.
I hope one day you will explain it to me.

When I mess up and disappoint you,
your anger never lasts
and you always forgive me.
I'm trying to forgive you.
I really am.

Not only did you give me life,
but you gave me a life worth living.
You've always been there for me.
You were my first friend,
and you are my biggest supporter.

That's why I hope you will understand
why I need to find my bio dad.
It isn't to hurt you, Mom.
It's to heal me.

Lately, we've had some gray skies,
but you are still my sunshine.

Aspen

Night Visitor

I'm climbing into bed
when I look up to see Mom
standing in the doorway.

She's holding the note
I just airmailed.

I thought you were sleeping, I say.

She swipes at a tear
and sits on the chair
beside my bed.

We all have a story, she says,
*there are parts we tell
and parts we keep hidden.*

She says she understands now
that after I was born
it stopped being her secret
and it became my story.

She reaches over and hugs me.
I'm sorry I lied to you.

When she unfolds my letter,
I notice the ski picture
of her and Luke tucked inside.

She looks at it one last time,
then hands it to me.

This is your biological father.
His name is Luke Zikas.
He's a good man.

She squeezes my hand,
Do what you feel is right.

When she reaches the door,
she turns back, *Aspen?*

Yeah, Mom?

Your DNA might not be what you expected
but you are beautiful
and smart,

and exactly
who you are supposed to be.

Sunshine and Shadow

Anticipation wakes me
before the mourning doves
outside my window get the chance.

In the bathroom, I get ready
for the biggest day of my life.
I try on a dozen outfits
but in the end, I settle
on black jeans and a tee.

I try to choke down
a piece of toast with jelly
but my stomach rebels.

When Sophie texts
On my way!
I grab my jacket
and my courage
and slip out the door.

While I wait for Sophie
beneath our towering oak,
the sun plays peek-a-boo
between copper leaves
and the enormity of
my situation hits me.

Today, I will meet the man
who created me and I'll learn
if we have a future together.

But for now,
for just a little while

l o n g e r,

I stand between
darkness and light,
sunshine and shadow,
knowing and not knowing.

Calling All Luck

You know that time
your hand slipped
from your water glass
and it fell to the floor
but bounced instead of breaking?

And the time
you pulled on jeans
you hadn't worn for weeks
and found twenty bucks in the pocket?

Or the time
a car barreled through the intersection
when you had the green light,
but somehow, it missed you by inches?

Yeah, I need that kind of luck today.

Countdown

Sophie's car sputters
down the street.

I look at her GPS.
15.3 miles to our destination.

When I learned my bio-dad
is practically my neighbor,
I felt like a fool all over again.

Have I seen Luke somewhere?
At the store?
At the library?
At a football game?

It's quiet inside the car
except for GPS Lady:
> *Keep right on Seafoam Drive*
> *Turn left on Palm Street.*

I bite my lip,
counting down the miles
while my mind taunts me
with wicked thoughts.

> 11.1 miles
> *He doesn't know you exist.*

> 8.9 miles
> *He'll hate you!*

7.4 miles
This is a mistake.

5.2 miles
You'll ruin his life.

2.4 miles
Keep the secret.

1.5 miles
Turn back now!

1 mile
It's not too late!

I panic when I hear,
in 900 feet, your destination is on the right.

Pull over, I cry, *I can't do this!*

Meltdown

Sophie pulls over
and turns toward me,
Talk to me, she says.

What if he doesn't believe me?
What if he doesn't like me?
What if he slams the door in my face?

Sophie answers,
He will.
He will.
He won't.

Promise? I ask.

Sophie promises
no matter what happens,
she will be here for me.

Charlie will be too.

Knowing
I have friends
to lean on gives me strength.

I suck in a deep breath.
Let's go.

Bad Timing

My phone rings.
It's my brother.

Seriously?
Now Cooper calls?

Hey Sis, he says,
How have you been?

I hesitate. *Fine.*

He senses something is wrong.
No, you're not!

I feel the tug of Dad's ring
on the chain around my neck.
I'm just thinking about Dad.

Yeah, I do that a lot too.

I tell him I can't talk now
but I have something important
to tell him later.

Call me anytime.
He hangs up.

I don't care what a stupid DNA test says,
Cooper may be my half-brother by blood
but he's my whole brother by heart.

You Have Arrived

Sophie drives the last 800 feet.

700
600
500
400
300
200
100

You've arrived at your destination.

I look out the window
at the white stucco house
with black shutters.

I have questions
I'm not sure how to ask.

There will be answers
I might not want to hear.

I think of the heroines
from the pages of my books,
Katniss Everdeen.
Scout Finch,
Hermione Granger.

They never shy away
from the challenges they face.

You've got this! Sophie says.

She's right.
I do.

This Is It

Sophie pulls
away from the curb.

She parks a block away,
her car idling,
waiting,
waiting,
for me to make my move.

I take a deep breath
hoping it will calm me.
But it doesn't work.
Calm isn't what I feel.
Nervous.
Worried.
Excited.
Scared.
Sick.
Yep, those are the feels.

When I take a few steps
across the lawn
I hear a loud noise.

I freeze.
Then relax.

It's just a guy
rolling a trash can
through a wide iron gate.

But wait!

I'd know that swagger anywhere.
It isn't a random guy,
it's Jaxon!

I turn around
and sprint back to the car
hoping he doesn't see me.

Shit
Shit
Shit

My frantic thoughts
mimicking the beat
of my feet
on the sidewalk.

I jump into Sophie's car.
Drive!

A Clean Getaway

Sophie jerks in her seat.
Jams her car in gear.
Punches the gas.

We sputter down the street,
a plume of exhaust chasing us.

What the hell is wrong? Sophie shouts
over the rumble of her engine.
You look like you've seen a ghost!

Worse, I say, my heart still racing.
I saw Jaxon!

So? Sophie shrugs.

*At Luke's house, Sophie,
he was rolling a trash can to the street,
like he lives there!*

Sophie takes the corner too fast.
Slams on the breaks.
Turns in her seat to look at me.

Are you freakin' kidding me right now?

Stealthy

Maybe Jaxon is doing a job for a neighbor, Sophie says.

I need to find out for sure.

We're like a pair
of stealth detectives
from a late-night TV show.

We take off on foot,
slipping past palm trees,
crouching behind cars,
hiding beside hedges.

We try to get close
to my bio-dad's house
without Jaxon seeing us.

We're across the street,
wedged between an RV
and a gray splintery fence
watching Jaxon rake leaves.

My nose itches, and I sneeze.
Shhhhh! Sophie whispers.
We inch farther back
into the shadows.

Jaxon looks up.

Does he see us? I ask Sophie.
I think he sees us! I panic.

But seconds later,
he's scooping leaves,
stuffing them into the trash can.

I don't think so. Sophie answers.

While we hide,
contemplating our next move,
a white truck pulls into the driveway.

A dark-haired man
sits behind the wheel.

Jaxon waves at him.

Hi Dad!

Don't Know Anything

I think I know so much.
I've studied
the phases of the moon.
I can diagram a sentence
and calculate
the hypotenuse
of a right triangle.
I can quote
Shakespeare,
Dante,
and Emily Bronte.
I know random facts
like the human brain
is made up of mostly fat
and honeybees
can be trained
to detect bombs.
I can puzzle out
a crossword,
Sudoku,
or jigsaw
with ease.
Why then,
didn't I figure out
that Jaxon Lee
is Jaxon Lee Zikas?
That my almost-boyfriend
is my half-brother?
Genes are born knowing.
Some of us have to learn
the hard way.

Back in the Bug

I've tugged on the past
like a child pulls at the yarn
of a delicate old sweater.

No matter how many times
her mother tells her not to tug,
she can't help herself.

In the end,
all she's left with
is a handful of what used to be.

What are you going to do? Sophie asks.

There's no going back.
I can't reknit the sweater.
I can't unknow the truth.

Let's go home, I sigh.

There's a time for words
and a time for silence.
Sophie always knows
what time it is.

She nods, starts her car.

I reach into my backpack
for my phone to call Charlie.
You'll never guess what happened.

Weighing My Options

It's late when Charlie knocks.
We talk about my options.

I know who my bio dad is,
is that enough?

If I don't try to meet him,
will I regret it?

If he'll have me,
do I want him in my life?
Mom says he's a good guy.

And what about Jaxon?
He's my brother!
Can I keep this secret from him?
From Cooper?
The secret that Mom kept from me?

If he doesn't know already,
is it my bio-dad's right
to know he has a daughter
and if so, is it my place to tell him?

And then there's my dad, Peter.
Would he want Luke to pick up
where he left off?

What does your heart say? Charlie asks.
You'll have to live with the decision you make.

If there's one thing
I've learned this past year,
it's that I'm strong.

I can handle things.
Big things.

I wrap my arms around Charlie
and rest my head on his chest.

My heart says, go!
Find your bio dad,
see if you have a future with him
and if you don't, you can handle it.

That's it then. Charlie kisses my forehead.
You have your answer.

I look up at him.
I have one more question.
Will you come with me?

My Story

After Charlie leaves,
I creep down the hall
past Mom's bedroom.

I think about waking her,
telling her what happened,
discussing my plans
to meet my bio-dad.

But I don't.

Sometimes you have to read
all the way to the end of a story
before you can share it with others.

This Way to Uncertainty

There's a steady drizzle
outside my window
when Charlie pulls up.

We don't need a GPS this time.
The address is saved
in my memory.

In a strange twist of fate,
Charlie's shuffled playlist
selects the song, *My Father's Eyes*.
We sing along with Eric Clapton,
the windshield wipers keeping time.

Luke's house is on the right, I say.

We pass Jaxon in his jeep.
I'm relieved to know he
won't be home when
I knock on his door.

Shocking news
should be taken
like medicine—
one dose at a time.

No Soliciting

I walk the cobblestone path,
past a garden of fuchsia,
through an arched gate,
and toward a sage green door
weathered from the sea air.

A NO SOLICITING sign
hangs from a rusty nail.

I wonder if my bio-dad
gets that a lot,
strangers showing up
on his doorstep
asking him to buy
what he doesn't need,
what he might not want.

Wait.
Am I a solicitor?

The Thing About Bravery

Standing on the porch,
I want to turn around and run
back to the safety of Charlie.

Then I remember
what he said last night
when I told him I was afraid.

He said being brave
doesn't mean you are fearless,
it means you have the strength
to overcome your fears.

I reach for Dad's ring
on the chain around my neck.

Charlie is right.

In the end
we only regret
the chances we didn't take.

Unwelcome?

A rolled-up newspaper.
Work boots.
A cracked flowerpot.

Of all the things on the porch,
something is missing—
a welcome mat.

What kind of person
doesn't put out
a welcome mat?

Before knocking,
I look back at Charlie
waiting in the car.

Two thumbs up!

My Move

With trembling hands,
I pump the door knocker
up and down,
up and down.

Dogs bark.
I hear a man's voice
shushing them.

Footsteps from inside
draw closer.
And closer.

They get louder.
And louder.

When Luke opens the door
my heart s k i t t e r s
in my chest.

Hi, my name is Aspen Deluca. Can we talk?

The Beginning

Our gazes lock.

Apprehension hangs
from my heart
like the hornet's nest
from the gable.

A flurry of worry.
A murmur of fear.

Deluca? he asks.

I nod.

I used to have a friend named Deluca, he says.

I know, that's why I'm here.

Luke stares at me,
How old are you, Aspen?

Bees buzz in the distance,
tiny wings beating fast
like my heart.

When I tell him I'm sixteen, he sighs,
sweeping a rough hand
through his wavy hair.

I sink to the porch step,
my legs like spaghetti al dente.
Luke sits down beside me.

I bite my lip, wondering
what he'll say next,
but he's quiet.

One one thousand
Two one thousand
Three one thousand

A few seconds feels like an eternity.

I didn't know, did you? I say,
filling the gap of silence
with my quivering voice.
He shakes his head. *Not until now.*

And then more silence.

I'm about to get up and go
when he stands
and opens his door.

A dimpled smile
dances across his face.
I think we have some catching up to do.

I breathe a calming mixture
of hope and possibility
into my lungs and

I step inside.

The Art of the Broken

There's a book in Dad's studio
about Kintsugi, the Japanese
art of mending broken
pottery with molten
gold. A cracked
vase is repaired, not
by disguising its imperfections
but by joyfully celebrating its brokenness.
With the visible golden seams, the vase is
made whole again and the scars become part
of its intended design. Strength and beauty can
be found in imperfection. Kintsugi is about
healing. It is not about forgetting what
was but going forward with what is.

I am Kintsugi.

AUTHOR'S NOTE

This is a work of fiction based on a true story—mine. DNA led me to my biological father, and after much soul-searching, I went to his home, stood on his doorstep, and introduced myself. I knew contacting him could have gone badly, but it was a chance I wanted to take. My biological father and his wife welcomed me. I affectionately call him my "Bonus Dad," and we are getting to know one another.

Jaxon's character is based on my half-brother. Unfortunately, he died before we could discover we were siblings. We unknowingly went to the same high school, passing one another in the halls as acquaintances.

Someone once asked me if I wished I had never taken a DNA test and stayed blissfully unaware of my paternity. I'll admit the struggle is real. I am still working through issues and probably always will be. Family secrets are like dominos. When they fall, they affect everyone in their path. But the answer to the question is an unequivocal no. I am worth the truth, and a messy truth is always better than a tidy lie.

ACKNOWLEDGMENTS

My heartfelt thanks to the amazing women in my writer's groups, Sharlee Glenn, Erin Cabatingan, Lezlie Evans, Linda Kimball, Carolyn Fisher, Kate Coombs, Linda Singleton, Bobi Martin, Linda Whalen, Verla Kay, Angelica Jackson, Connie Goldsmith, and Melody DeLeon, for their thoughtful suggestions and encouragement along the way. To my online support group, DNA NPE, where a shoulder and good advice are always just a click away. A multitude of thank-yous to my agent, Tracy Marchini, who believed in Aspen's story from the very beginning. My love to my children, Boston and Olivia, whose lives were also affected by my DNA discovery, and to Cindy and Laurie, my half-sisters by blood but my whole sisters by heart. And last but never least, my undying gratitude to my husband, Dave, who held me up when life got hard and encouraged my therapy through poetry. You are all precious gifts.

ABOUT THE AUTHOR

Danna Smith is a poet and award-winning author of over twenty books for children. A pencil was her favorite toy when she was young as she became fascinated with writing and wordplay. *The Complete Book of Aspen* is her debut novel based on her true experience. Today, Danna's favorite toy is a keyboard. She currently lives and creates at her home in beautiful northern California wine country. You can find her books at www.dannasmithbooks.com and pop over to her poetry blog at www.poetrypop.com.

AN EXPLANATION OF
POETIC FORMS

The majority of the novel, *The Complete Book of Aspen*, is written in narrative verse. Here is a look at other poetic forms used by the author.

CONCRETE POEMS: In a concrete poem (also called a shape poem), the poet arranges words in the subject's shape to enrich or add to the meaning of the poetry. The concrete poems in this book include the following:

Mad Scientist: This poem is written in the shape of a lightbulb to represent Sophie's love of science.

Sunshine: Shaped like the sun, this poem represents the warmth of the relationship between Aspen and her mother and their song.

Curiosity: This poem is in the shape of a question mark to represent Aspen's unanswered questions.

R.I.P.: This poem is in the shape of a cross to represent death.

Heart to Heart: Shaped like a heart, this poem represents the heartfelt talk between Aspen and her deceased father.

Loves Me Loves Me Not: Shaped like a flower and plucked petals, this poem represents the words Aspen chants about Charlie and their troubled relationship.

Hello, Dad, Are You There? This poem is shaped like a candlestick to represent Aspen's memory of her dad and his pottery.

The Bad Thing about Running: This poem is written in the shape of a circle to represent the problems Aspen can't escape.

Observation: Shaped like a Double Helix, this poem mirrors the connection to Aspen's break up with Charlie and her issues regarding her DNA.

Happy Birthday to Me: This poem is in the shape of a balloon to celebrate Aspen's birthday.

The Art of the Broken: This vase-shaped poem represents Aspen's bond with her father through pottery and her ability to understand, repair, and embrace her brokenness.

FOUND POEM
To the Lady in the Store Looking at DNA Tests is a found poem. This type of poem is made by finding words from printed material such as a newspaper, a page in a book, or a song and rearranging them to form an original poem. This poem was found from the words in a popular DNA mission statement.

HAIKU

The poem **Storm** is a Haiku, a Japanese form of poetry consisting of three lines written to be read in one breath. The first and the third lines contain five syllables, and the middle line has seven syllables for a total of seventeen syllables. Haiku is written in incomplete sentences, usually speaks of a moment in nature, and ends with a shift of perspective or enlightenment.

HOW-TO POEM

How to find a Bio-Dad in Five Steps is a How-To Poem. This type of poem creatively explains the process, line by line, of how to do something. The poem can be serious or silly, rhymed, or unrhymed.

LIST POEMS

A list poem is just that, a list of items, ideas, or people. List poems usually have a few lines at the beginning and the end with the list in the middle. Most list poems end with a surprise or a "twist" to the list. The list poems included in *The Complete Book of Aspen* are:

RSVP
Dead Phone
Keepsakes

PREFIX POEM

The poem, **Blood** is based on features of a Prefix Poem although not all words used are prefixes. It is loosely modeled after the poem *Trans* by Idra Novey, in which she starts with a prefix for the title and the first section and then builds upon the poem's meaning with additional sections.

RHYME

There are three basic types of rhymed stanzas, Perfect Rhyme (all end words rhyme exactly), Slant Rhyme (all end rhymes are not exact rhymes but sound similar), and Internal Rhyme (rhymes are placed in the middle of the same line of poetry, not at the end). The rhymed poetry in this book includes:

Lunch in the Library: slant rhyme stanza.
4 Reasons Why Charlie is the 1: perfect rhyme.

SENRYU

The poem, *Ice Cream,* is a Senryu. Haiku and Senryu are often confused with one another. They are both three-line poems with a 5/7/5 syllable count, but the subject and tone are different. Haiku is about nature and seasons with a reverent tone, while the haiku's cousin, senryu, is about human nature (characteristics, behavior, emotions, traits), often humorous.

SKINNY POEM

It Could be a Lie is a Skinny Poem. "Skinnys" convey a vivid image with as few words as possible and generally reflect serious concerns facing humankind. They consist of 11 lines. Lines 1 and 11 can be any length, and line 11 must use the same words from line 1 (but they can be rearranged). Lines 2, 6, and 10 must be identical. All lines except for 1 and 11 must only be one word long.

TRIVERSEN POEM

In a triversen (also known as a verset), each stanza is composed of a single sentence, broken into three lines. The poem is usually unrhymed and should add up to 18 lines (6 stanzas). The poems, *Party Crasher* and *The F Word* are triversen poems.

WHERE I'M FROM POEM

Aspen's poem, *Dear Charlie*, is modeled after the classic poem *Where I'm From* by George Ella Lyon. This form of poetry allows the reader into the life of the speaker. It helps the reader understand who the speaker is and where they are from.